Shadows of the Sorcerers

Chronicles of the Library of Sorcery

Shadows of the Sorcerers

Chronicles of the Library of Sorcery

Joan Marie Verba

FTL Publications
Minneapolis, Minnesota

Copyright © 2024 by Joan Marie Verba

FTL Publications
P O Box 22693
Minneapolis, MN 55345-0363
www.ftlpublications.com
mail@ftlpublications.com

Cover designed by Getcovers

Printed in the United States of America

ISBN 978-1-936881-86-4

Acknowledgments

I wish to extend my sincere thanks to Elizabeth Rowan Keith for her valuable advice and encouragement as I wrote this novel.

About the Author

Joan Marie Verba is an autistic author, publisher, and web developer with a bachelor's degree in physics. She was an associate instructor of astronomy for one year. She has worked as a computer programmer, web developer, editor, publisher, and social media manager. An experienced writer, she is the author of fiction and nonfiction books plus numerous short stories and articles. Her novels have received the Mom's Choice Award® and the Scribe Award. She is a member of the Science Fiction and Fantasy Writers Association and the International Association of Media Tie-in Writers.

To find out more about Joan, or to sign up for her newsletter, go to her website at https://joanmarieverba.com.

Chapter 1

Marlys agreed with Thorne that they needed to call for a council of sorcerers to deal with the threat before someone was killed. Gathering her sorcerous strength, Marlys reached out to all the central locations in the continent, including the Library of Sorcery.

"Pardon the interruption," Marlys said, "but we have a serious incident in Briarhill that requires everyone's attention."

"A sorcerers' council?" Lindra, the High Sorcerer at Cloverdell, asked.

"Yes," Marlys said. "The town of Riverglen was looted, and by Edwina's account, all indications are that there are rogue sorcerers at work."

"Rogue sorcerers?" Genevieve, the Head Librarian at the Library of Sorcery, chimed in. "We've had none of those here in centuries."

Thorne, who had taken a chair to sit next to Marlys, touched Marlys on the sleeve. "May I?"

Marlys nodded. Thorne had been the High Sorcerer of Goldenvalley before Marlys, and currently had the title of Senior Sorcerer of Goldenvalley.

Thorne addressed Genevieve. "They're rare here, too. The last incident I dealt with was nearly 40 years ago."

"Here in the Library District," Genevieve said, "we keep a close watch on the towns and villages for those who can perform household spells. It would be nearly impossible for any of them to become a sorcerer without our knowledge, much less one exercising powers self-taught."

"We do our best," Thorne replied, "but we don't have adequate numbers to visit every area regularly, and it is possible for youngsters bent on secret havoc to hide their powers from us."

"Whatever the case," Marlys said, "it's a challenge we have to meet, and quickly. Edwina already sent sorcerers from her region to investigate. They weren't able to locate the perpetrators. They remain on alert. We are going to have to help scour the region in greater numbers, as soon as possible."

"Oh, does that mean we have to postpone my celebration?" Janna, at the Valleyview training center, had just come into her powers. Marlys had scheduled the recognition ceremony for the next day.

Before Marlys could answer, Genevieve said, "Don't postpone your celebration. I'll come, and Blair is waving his hand volunteering to accompany me. I want to see this."

"If you can arrange to transport us to Briarhill," Niquelle, the High Sorcerer at Silvervale said, "I and some of my more experienced sorcerers are willing to join you. But we're so distant it would take the power of a Librarian to take us there."

"I'd be happy to do that," Genevieve said.

"I can come with sorcerers, too," Ware, High Sorcerer of Woodlands, added, "again, if a Librarian can take us there."

Genevieve turned her head. "Blair says he can transport you."

"I don't wish to miss Janna's celebration," Thorne said, "but you are going to need me, since all of you are pledged to not to harm other sorcerers, and I have an exception for rogues."

"There are other ways of handling rogue sorcerers that do not involve harming them," Genevieve said. "By all means, stay for the celebration."

"I intend to come at my earliest opportunity, however," Thorne said.

"I will, too," Marlys said.

"As for me," Janna said, "I'm willing to postpone my ceremony if it means catching these culprits all the sooner. In fact, I'd love to join you and test my powers."

"You are far from ready to deal with this," Thorne said.

"Maybe," Janna said, undaunted, "but you at least need someone my age to observe in case there are rogue sorcerers after your time that my generation needs to deal with."

Marlys held up a hand to forestall an extended argument. "We'll take this under consideration later. Meanwhile, thanks to all those volunteering to help. We'll see you here tomorrow, Janna."

"We will keep you, and everyone else, informed of our progress," Genevieve said.

Marlys nodded. "We'd be grateful for that. Thank you, and good evening."

When Marlys entered the training center at Valleyview at the age of sixteen, Janna had been her primary tormentor. Because Marlys had suspended her in time, along with all the other sorcerers and apprentices in Goldenvalley in that era, for twelve years, Marlys was now thirty, and Janna, nineteen. Since Janna had been released from the time-bind, Janna had largely abandoned her bullying ways. Even so, Marlys found her youthful experiences hard to forget. She did her best to carry on the tradition of celebrating an apprentice's awakening of sorcery, but she found there was no joy in her heart for arranging this for Janna.

Nonetheless, the next morning after breakfast, Marlys stood at the entrance of the Goldenvalley fortress, warmly welcoming the region's sorcerers and apprentices as they arrived. Behind her stood three other Librarians—holding that title since their sorcerous powers had been enhanced at the Library of Sorcery: Serena, Tir, and Rochelle, her most stalwart allies. Thorne stood to one side at the bottom of the front steps, greeting all the guests. Marlys noticed an exceptional warmth to the ones who had served with her when she was High Sorcerer.

At last, carts from Valleyview began to appear out of distance-shortening spells. Among them was a cart carrying Elspeth, who had been Marlys's sorcerer-trainer, Janna, and Kelsie. Although the same age as Janna, Kelsie's sorcery had not yet awakened. Marlys retained a wariness about Kelsie as well, since Kelsie had eagerly joined Janna in earlier abusive behavior toward Marlys, though Kelsie, too, had settled into more moderate ways of late.

Once an apprentice from the fortress had stepped forward to take the cart, Elspeth, Janna, and Kelsie climbed off. As with everyone else at the event, they had dressed in their finest outfits: elegant, embroidered dresses, with silver and gold piping, glittering with jewels. Thorne ran forward to meet them, embracing each in turn. They walked to the fortress and up the stairs, pausing when they drew even with Marlys.

Marlys faced Janna with a smile and all the warmth she could muster. Janna had an oval face and short, straight brown hair. "Congratulations, Janna, on awakening your sorcery. Make your way to the audience room and I'll meet you there when everyone has arrived."

Janna said nothing, but nodded and grinned. She walked inside with Elspeth, Kelsie, and Thorne.

Tir leaned toward Marlys and spoke in her ear. "At least she's behaving herself."

"Elspeth says she gets into minor mischief at times, but on the whole, takes her responsibility seriously."

"In other words, we're still on guard with her," Serena said.

"Naturally," Marlys said.

Once everyone had gathered in the audience room, Marlys made her way over to Janna. She and Marlys and Thorne, as arranged, walked with her to the dais. Janna stood in the center, facing the crowd, with Marlys standing on Janna's left and Thorne standing at Janna's right.

Marlys put an arm around Janna's shoulder and addressed the assembly. "Please join me in welcoming Sorcerer Janna."

The guests cheered enthusiastically. Tir provided sparkling lights. Others conjured snowflakes, which evaporated before reaching the ground.

Everyone gravitated to the tables of food set out near the walls. The sun shone brightly through the stained glass windows and the beams brightened the floor. Tir, Rochelle, and other musicians among the sorcerers struck up a tune. Janna led the dances.

When their energy was spent, all drifted into small groups, conversing. Marlys, as was her obligation, ambled over to Janna, surrounded by Kelsie, Elspeth, and Thorne.

"Your turn next, Kelsie." Janna took a swig from her cider mug.

"I will when I'm ready," Kelsie said with a smile.

Janna gave Kelsie a playful shove. "You're never ready."

"I'm happy using household spells," Kelsie said, "and watching the rest of you do your sorcery."

Thorne let out a breath. "There was some reason you came to a center of sorcery."

Kelsie shrugged. "I had nothing else to do. I didn't want to get married, and I didn't want to farm or learn a trade. I just wanted to have fun, and I could do household spells."

"You're wasting your talents," Thorne said.

"Besides, if you become a sorcerer, we could do sorcery together," Janna said. "That would be even more fun!"

Kelsie's smile never faded. "I'll think it over."

Thorne shook her head sadly.

"Until you're ready," Marlys said to Kelsie, "you're welcome to remain as an apprentice."

"Yes, and you won't have to go through torture to awaken your sorcery," Celestine said pointedly, looking meaningfully at Thorne. "All Janna had to do was break through a crucible."

Marlys had not noticed Celestine's approach, but could not help but catch the implication. Before Marlys, Throne imposed brutal methods to awaken sorcery, thinking this was the only way.

Thorne stared back at Celestine, but did not take the bait.

Ignoring her elders, Janna turned back to Kelsie, "Make up your mind soon. Otherwise, you'll be as old as Marlys before you become a sorcerer."

"That would not be so bad," Celestine said kindly. "I've heard of sorcerers who waited several years before trying to awaken their sorcery."

"From what I understand," Marlys said, "there have been apprentices at the Library of Sorcery who waited until they were in their 30s or 40s, though most become sorcerers well before then."

"I think that long before that, Kelsie will want to join in," Elspeth said.

"Besides," Kelsie said, "I'll know all the spells before I become a sorcerer, and not have to learn them after."

Thorne chuckled. "There are too many spells for that. We're all still learning ourselves."

"You'll know a great many of them, though," Marlys said.

At that moment, an image of Genevieve appeared in the room. "Marlys, can you join us?"

The room quieted.

"Yes, I can join you," Marlys said. "What have you found?"

"Nothing, so far," Genevieve said. "We've scoured every part of the towns and countryside around Riverglen and there's no sign of the intruders, whoever they are. Our thought is to bring more sorcerers, spread them out so that each sorcerer is within sight of each other, and cover the widest area in case they return."

"They will," Thorne said. "You can count on it."

"I was about to ask if you would come, too," Genevieve said, "since you are the only living sorcerer we know of with experience of rogues."

"I'm only too glad to help," Thorne said.

"Do you have an idea of how many sorcerers you need from Goldenvalley?" Marlys asked.

"Just bring whoever and how many you believe can join in the task," Genevieve said.

"We'll use the locator spell to find you and be there shortly," Marlys said.

"Thank you," Genevieve said. Her image faded.

Marlys looked around. "Volunteers? We'll need to change from our formal clothes quickly."

"We have time," Thorne said. "I doubt they will show themselves until dusk."

"We're willing to help," Skye said. "But a lot of us don't know quite what to do."

"Then stay here with me," Celestine said. "They may need us to send supplies or contact other regions for aid."

Marlys nodded. "That's a sound plan."

Rochelle started to move toward an exit. "I'm bringing weapons."

"You can't use those on sorcerers," Thorne said.

"Weapons have other uses," Rochelle said, "and they may not all be sorcerers."

"Very well," Thorne conceded.

"I can't go," Nessa said, "I'm still under banishment in the other regions."

Zaria took a deep breath. "My banishment was just lifted. Time to test it. Besides, I can attack sorcerers."

Janna raised a hand. "I haven't been pledged yet."

"We were getting to that," Marlys said.

"You're too inexperienced, to go, anyway," Thorne said.

"Take her," Elspeth said. "and she'll get the experience."

Thorne threw Marlys a look that Marlys knew showed Thorne remained skeptical, and said, "She should stay here. But I agree we should avoid pledging her not to harm other sorcerers until we know what we're dealing with. We may need her in the future."

Marlys turned to Janna. "I agree with Thorne that we can wait to pledge you. But I agree with Elspeth that you may go for the experience."

Janna grinned and rubbed her hands together.

"But you will stay with either Thorne or me, and your purpose is to observe, not act," Marlys said.

Janna responded with a smug smile that told Marlys that Janna intended to disobey at the earliest opportunity. But Marlys kept that thought to herself. Janna might still be useful.

All who wanted to go changed into outdoor gear within minutes. Every fortress kept a store of extra clothes; Janna soon found an outfit. The other volunteers were Marlys, Thorne, Serena, Tir, Rochelle, and Zaria.

Rochelle strode toward Marlys armed with a short sword in a scabbard belted around her waist and a round shield slung over her back. She carried a leather jerkin, which she handed to Marlys. "Here, put this on. It's spelled for extra protection."

Glancing around, Marlys saw that the other volunteers, save Thorne, had also donned protective clothing: thick gloves, caps, vests.

Thorne had settled for only an outdoor shirt, pants, and boots. "No confidence in your sorcery, I see."

"No confidence in our opponents, rather," Rochelle said.

Marlys had already cast the locator spell to determine Genevieve's current location. Now she cast the transportation spell. "Ready?"

The volunteers nodded.

"May the protection of the Bright Beings go with you," Celestine called as they exited.

"Thank you, we'll need it," Marlys said as she followed the others.

Chapter 2

Marlys and the others emerged near a road winding through a sparsely wooded area. To the southeast, Marlys could see the town of Riverglen in the distance. Sorcerers from Goldenvalley, Silvervale, Woodlands, Briarhill, and the Library District surrounded her.

Genevieve stepped toward Marlys. "Thank you for coming. We were about to spread out."

"How far did you have in mind?" Marlys asked.

"Far enough so that you can see someone on either side of you within easy calling distance," Edwina said.

Marlys nodded and gestured to the others. "All right, let's go."

"Briarhill sorcerers," Edwina called, "fill in the space between here and Riverglen, and set up watch within the town as well."

A group of sorcerers separated from the others and complied.

Janna started to walk toward Thorne.

"Stay by me," Marlys said.

Janna turned to Marlys. "I thought I'd stay with Thorne."

"Thorne and I will stay in sight of each other," Marlys said. "You won't be too far away from her."

"Do as Marlys says," Thorne said, and ambled away.

Marlys walked through the short grasses and clover between the trees. The sun was lowering, the sky was clear. She saw a fox scamper through the grass in front of her. Birds chirped, perched high in the trees. A fresh, warm breeze played with the leaves.

When Marlys felt she stood a comfortable distance away from Thorne, she stopped. Janna, trailing behind her, halted and faced Thorne.

Looking to her other side, Marlys spotted Tir standing among the shadows of the trees.

"What do we do now?" Janna asked.

"We wait and watch," Marlys said.

"That sounds boring," Janna said.

"In a watch," Marlys said, "one is supposed to look around, noticing the height of the trees, the rocks among the grasses, and other details of one's surroundings, so that if any one thing goes out of place, it is immediately apparent."

Janna scratched her chin and started to look around.

Marlys, in her observations, noticed Rochelle at a farther distance, pacing. The road remained in view. She could spot the outlying buildings of the town and a sorcerer on patrol there.

After a time, Janna said, "Do I have to stay in place or can I walk around a little?"

"By all means, stretch your legs, but don't go far."

Janna crossed her arms in front of her and walked in a circle around Marlys. To her credit, Janna scanned the area the entire time.

The sun had nearly reached the horizon when Janna spoke again. "Do we have to remain quiet or can we talk to each other?"

"We're also listening for any sounds of movement that are out of place," Marlys said, "so we need to be reasonably quiet."

Janna shrugged.

Marlys caught a motion in Thorne's direction. Thorne pointed to a nearby clearing between trees where a figure stood. Marlys had just looked in that direction moments before and saw nothing.

Thorne gestured at Marlys and slowly crept toward the figure. Marlys faced Janna, put a finger to her lips, and motioned to Janna to come with her. Out of the corner of her eye, she saw Tir moving quietly, and ahead of her, Rochelle coming forward.

The intruder, seemingly aware of being spotted, began to move.

Immediately, Thorne cast a spell, freezing the figure in time.

No longer in need of stealth, all five sorcerers ran to the figure.

When Thorne stood within arm's reach, she said, "Argent!"

"What?" Marlys said.

Tir cast a lighting spell. The area brightened as if it were noon on a sunny day.

Thorne turned to Marlys. "The rogue sorcerer I banished long ago."

"Are you sure?" Tir asked.

Thorne stepped closer to the man, carefully taking note of his features. "He's older, yes, but it's him." She pointed. "V-shaped notch on the right ear. Hairy mole on the neck. Scar above the left eyebrow. Couldn't be anyone else."

Marlys felt chilled. "You said you banished him to the island worlds."

Thorne faced her. "I did. I watched him go through myself before I closed the portal."

By this time, apparently attracted by the light, other sorcerers had come running.

When Marlys saw Genevieve, she said, "Genevieve, is there any record of someone returning from the island worlds?"

"No, never." Genevieve scrutinized Argent closely. "You mean this one has found a way back?"

"Or someone else found the way for him," Tir said. "Edwina told us there were other raiders at Riverglen."

"I haven't seen anyone else." Genevieve looked up and called. "Blair! Do you see anything?"

Marlys followed Genevieve's gaze and spotted Blair perched at the top of a tall tree in the distance.

"No," Blair said. "No one but sorcerers we know of in sight."

Marlys turned to Genevieve again. "What do we do with Argent?"

"I know." Before anyone could say or do anything else, Thorne cast the spell to open the portal to the island worlds and at the same time canceled the time-bind. Argent was sucked in, and Thorne closed the portal.

Marlys and the others had to anchor themselves sorcerously to the ground to keep from being propelled through the portal themselves.

Genevieve turned and said—amazingly calmly, Marlys thought—to Thorne, "Why did you do that? We could have questioned him and found out how he got here."

Thorne snorted. "As if he would tell us. I've dealt with him before. He admits nothing. He confesses nothing. He regrets nothing. We're best rid of him."

"Until he comes back," Tir said.

"If he comes back," Thorne said. "Even if he did have the wit to find out how to come back himself, which I doubt, we can just send him back again."

"I don't think that's a sound long-term plan," Niquelle said.

"Well, for now, at least, he's gone," Thorne said.

Meanwhile, Tir had been testing the ground with his foot. He knelt.

"Something?" Marlys asked him.

Tir looked up. "I remember reading accounts of the sorcerous wars. The aggressors would dig shelters in the ground, like root cellars, to hide in, and then come up unexpectedly and attack. I think there's an entry close by."

Rochelle reached down and patted Tir on the side. "Let me. It's possible to rig a trap door so that it hurts anyone who tries to open it."

Tir scrambled to his feet and stepped back. "It's all yours."

As Rochelle searched, Marlys turned to Thorne. "Did Argent have an underground hideout at the time you opposed him?"

"No," Thorne said. "He was out in the open."

Genevieve stepped next to Rochelle. "Concealing spell. Let me cancel it."

Rochelle remained still as Genevieve cast her spell. Tir's light revealed a wooden door set in a stone frame flat on the ground. The door had an iron ring at one end.

"Wood preserved by sorcery," Niquelle said.

Rochelle positioned herself at the hinges, reached down and over, and slowly pulled.

Tir leaned to one side to check the opening. "No traps that I can see or sense. There's a sorcerous light inside."

Slowly, Rochelle pulled the door all the way open, and set it on the ground.

Marlys peered inside. "Stone steps. I don't hear the sounds of movement."

"We can't be sure we won't be ambushed." Rochelle pulled her shield from her back and set it over an arm. "I'll go first."

After descending a few steps, Rochelle crouched, ducked her head and looked around. Raising her head again, she said, "No one there I can see. The place is huge. It's more than a root cellar."

Genevieve craned her neck. "Blair is still scanning the area from above. I'd suggest that no more than a dozen of us go down there and look around. The rest can keep watch up here."

"We'll stay," Ware said.

Genevieve turned to Marlys. "The Goldenvalley contingent is mainly Librarians. I'd say all of you and I will explore and the rest remain. If either senses trouble, the other can come to their aid."

Marlys nodded and heard sounds of agreement.

Rochelle led the way as the others followed her down the stairs.

When they reached the floor of the cavern, Marlys looked around. The ceiling rose high above her. This room, cut from stone, was roughly circular. Circular openings in the walls indicated exits and tunnels. Before them stood a round stone table ringed by raised stone seats.

Tir raised his hands, waved them, and put a finger to his lips. He crept toward one of the circular exits and pointed. The others clustered around him. Marlys heard voices in the distance, accompanied by the clatter of plates and cutlery.

"Dinner?" Thorne said in a low voice.

Marlys nodded.

"What now?" Tir murmured.

At that moment, a strong wind blew within the chamber. Marlys and the others had to use anchoring spells to keep from being blown over. Turning, Marlys saw a portal open. A man stepped out, and the portal closed.

"Argent!" Thorne called.

"Ha! Thorne!" Argent answered. "Thought you were rid of me?"

Thorne cast a pushing spell, slamming Argent against a far wall.

To Marlys's surprise, Argent simply straightened, brushed himself off, and shouted, "Attack!" The word echoed in the chamber.

Genevieve made a motion to cast a spell, but before it could land, Argent sorcerously thrust her against a wall. She hit her head and slumped to the floor, unconscious.

Men poured out of the openings in the stone walls. Marlys's company suddenly found themselves beset. Resisting the forces pushing at her, Marlys pressed her way toward Genevieve, knelt, and began the healing process.

Rochelle stood next to her, weapon ready, and called, "You tend to Genevieve. I'll defend you."

As Marlys worked, she could hear a cacophony of sound: striking, clashing, shrieking. Flickering lights. She felt herself pushed around as the edge of offensive spells buffeted her. Arrows and spears hit the wall above her and to either side. She felt the swoosh of Rochelle's sword and shield deflecting them.

"These shouldn't be reaching us," Rochelle yelled above the din. "Our defensive spells should be protecting us."

"Get out of here," Marlys said. "I'll follow when I can."

"Not leaving you," Rochelle said.

Marlys silently prayed to the Bright Beings to keep her going just long enough to revive Genevieve. She could feel the healing taking place in the other woman, but knew she had to complete the task to avoid lasting injury.

The uproar in the room grew significantly quieter. Suddenly, Marlys glanced to one side and saw Blair, not Rochelle, standing next to her. Facing Genevieve again, Marlys saw Genevieve's eyes flutter open.

Blair reached down and pulled them up. "We're going. Ow!"

Marlys saw that Blair had cast a transportation spell and stepped inside with him.

They emerged in the Goldenvalley audience room.

"Take her!" Blair called.

Celestine and Rochelle rushed forward to help Genevieve.

"Blair," Tir said, "I'm going to remove your shirt so I can heal that arrow wound."

"Yes, please do!" Blair said. The arrow shaft still protruded from his back.

"Marlys, are you all right?" Niquelle asked.

"Yes," Marlys said, looking around. "Is everyone here?"

"Everyone accounted for from Silvervale, Woodlands, and Goldenvalley," Niquelle said. "I presume the Briarhill sorcerers are reinforcing their borders."

Astrid rushed over. "I just spoke with Edwina over the sorcerous channels. They've cast spells of protection around Riverglen and dispatched sorcerers to other towns in Briarhill to protect them."

Ware joined Niquelle and Marlys. "We have to get back to our regions. We need to take steps to be sure we're not attacked."

"Nessa is spreading the news elsewhere, including the Library of Sorcery," Astrid said.

"I'll take the Silvervale and Woodlands sorcerers home," Zaria offered.

"Thank you," Marlys said.

When they were gone, Marlys looked around the room. Genevieve had been settled in a lounge chair. Lyra gave her a cup of tea. Blair straddled a chair. A bloody shirt with a tear in the back had been draped over a chair next to him. An arrow with a bloody tip had been placed on the chair seat. Tir arranged a blanket over Blair's shoulders and handed him a mug of steaming cider.

Elsewhere, Elspeth sat facing Thorne.

When Marlys approached, Thorne said, "One of those rogues gave me a black eye. I'm healing it."

Turning to her left, Marlys saw Voni sitting in front of Janna, holding one of Janna's hands.

Voni nodded at Janna. "You've done well healing your hand."

Janna looked up at Marlys and grinned. "I broke a couple of bones in my hand, but the others looked worse." She extended her free hand. A piece of jewelry had lay in a palm. "And I snagged a prize!"

Marlys leaned forward. The object reminded her of the face of a weasel with bared teeth. Two small pearls formed the eyes.

"It's spelled," Janna said. "I can feel it."

"What does it do?" Marlys asked.

Janna shook her head. "Don't know. Everyone I saw wore one. They seemed to use it as a pin to keep a shirt or a cloak fastened."

"Mind if I hold it?" Marlys asked.

Janna extended her hand. "Take it."

Marlys carefully took it with a thumb and forefinger and placed it in the palm of her hand. She closed her eyes and did her best to read it. Janna was right; it was spelled. But she had no more idea of what it did than Janna.

Serena ambled over. "What is it?"

Marlys held up her hand. "A prize Janna snagged."

"Oh, yes, I saw those brutes wearing those." Serena turned to Janna. "I was too busy keeping them from killing us to think of snatching one. Good work, Janna."

Tir came into view carrying the arrow. "This is what hit Blair in the shoulder blade. It's spelled. Probably how it got past his sorcerous protection."

Serena pointed at the jeweled pin Marlys held. Janna nodded and Marlys handed it over. After studying it, she handed it back to Janna. "I can't tell what it does, either."

Voni finished healing Janna's hand, released it, and turned to Marlys. "What do we do now, Marlys?"

Marlys took a long breath. "I honestly don't know."

Chapter 3

By the time Zaria returned, the wounded had been treated and healed. Marlys stood near a table and asked the sorcerers who felt well enough to discuss the next steps. No one declined. As everyone moved toward the table to join Marlys, Celestine gathered apprentices, who returned with trays of food and beverages. Genevieve left the lounge chair and took a seat at the table. Tir had found a fresh shirt for Blair. Rochelle's leather jerkin showed blood spatter, but she seemed fine, as did other sorcerers with bloodstains on their sleeves or vests.

When all had been seated—sorcerers together, apprentices hovering nearby—Marlys turned to Genevieve.

"Has anything like this happened before?" she asked.

Genevieve shook her head. "Not since the sorcerous wars."

"No one has ever returned from being banished to the island worlds before, that I can confirm," Blair said.

"We have to strike back quickly," Thorne said, "before they increase their numbers beyond what we can defend."

"We can't even defend against the numbers they have now," Astrid said.

"Precisely my point," Thorne said. "It can only get worse."

"How do we know that there will be more?" Genevieve said. "Perhaps this is all they have."

"We don't know," Thorne said, "but we can't naively presume we saw all of them."

"How many were there?" Voni asked. "Does anyone know?"

She was answered by murmured "nos" and head shaking.

"I was too busy to count!" Zaria said.

"A few dozen, perhaps," Rochelle said, "but not hundreds. Before I apprenticed as a sorcerer, I trained to be part of a magistrate's patrol. What we experienced reminded me more of a barroom brawl than a battle. Our numbers became roughly even once the sorcerers from Woodlands and Silvervale came to our aid."

"Armies are a thing of the past," Genevieve said. "No one has fought a battle since the sorcerous wars. We've worked hard to keep the peace since then."

"We can't be sure that the conflict won't escalate into a war," Thorne said.

"We may have been bested because we weren't expecting a brawl," Rochelle said, "and they showed no signs of being trained fighters, either. I doubt that they could organize an army."

"However many they have," Blair said, "how to we oppose them? We barely escaped with our lives."

"Only Janna, Zaria, and I have the ability to strike at sorcerers without destroying ourselves," Thorne said.

"But were they all sorcerers?" Rochelle said. "We were facing offensive spells, yes, but a lot of them were attacking with fists and weapons."

"Some of those weapons, if not all of them, spelled," Blair pointed out.

Rochelle nodded. "Undoubtedly sorcerers were supplying them."

"Our spells weren't always effective," Serena said. "The protective spells, for instance, only partially worked. As for offensive spells, I tried the knockout spell right away, and to no avail."

Marlys heard others say some variation of "Yes, I tried that, too," or "Didn't work for me."

Serena reached over in Janna's direction and lifted the jewelry piece Janna had placed on the table. "You said that you saw everyone wearing one of these?"

"Yes," Janna said, nodding.

Serena looked around at the others. "I think we just discovered what this does. Or one of the things it does, anyway: protecting the wearer against knockout spells, at least, possibly other spells, too."

"I could push people away with sorcery," Tir said. "That spell worked, at least."

Serena slid the jeweled pin back to Janna. "Yes, I tried any number of spells, and some worked, or else we wouldn't be here."

"The transportation spell, most of all, worked," Blair said.

"They can't duplicate that, they aren't Librarians," Zaria said.

"We don't know that," Rochelle said. "That is, they may not be Librarians as we understand the term, but Argent, at least, can return from the island worlds, something none of the rest of us know how to do. He has great sorcerous strength, even if we don't know the origins of that strength. He may not know the transportation spell, but he may have the power to cast it, if he learns it, and he is, by all admissions, self-taught."

"That's alarming," Blair said.

"Another difference," Tir said, "is that his comrades were all men."

"All?" Voni said.

Blair nodded solemnly. "Even in all the confusion, that's the one thing I am certain of."

"Anyone who heard him in the old days remembers him pouring contempt on sorcerers and how we were all women," Thorne said. "Sorcerers ought to be men, he would say. That's what was wrong with this world, according to him, and he would fix that."

"I've never heard any man here say that," Tir said.

His statement was met with sounds of agreement from others in the room.

"In the Library District, young men generally aspire to prestigious occupations such as ranchers, barkeeps, crafters, magistrates, or magistrate deputies," Blair said. "Sorcery is considered a necessary but hazardous vocation, and most are relieved that anyone does it, regardless of gender."

"Here sorcery still has the reputation of being harsh and grueling work," Tir said, "and only the most determined seek it out."

"This is unquestionably one of those times when that is true," Elspeth said.

Marlys turned to Genevieve again. "We need to make a plan."

"We do indeed," Genevieve said. "Do you have any suggestions as to where to start?"

Marlys expected that the great Librarians would have an answer for everything. She could not help feeling disappointed that she had been asked for a plan.

"With all due respect to our High Sorcerer," Throne said, "Marlys, you're too soft-hearted for a task such as this."

A burst of laughter erupted in the room. Apparently most Goldenvalley sorcerers disagreed with Thorne.

Thorne continued, undaunted. "Have you ever killed a person?"

"Have you?" Marlys asked.

"No, but I don't doubt I could if needed. Could you?"

"Before and after I came here for sorcerer training, I hunted for dinner," Marlys said.

"Killing a person is different," Thorne said.

"And therefore to be avoided at all costs," Marlys said.

"And if it can't be avoided?" Thorne said.

"In my patrol training," Rochelle said, "my trainer said that no one can tell who will act or who will freeze until the moment happens. The mildest recruit can become fierce, and the most determined recruit could quail."

"Do you remember two years ago when you and I stood on the road to the fortress?" Marlys asked Thorne. "I was ready to stop you even if it meant sacrificing both of us. That should answer your question."

Thorne took in a long breath and exhaled slowly, but said nothing in response.

"Besides, I am oath-bound not to harm another sorcerer," Marlys said. "Attacking one, as you found, requires an extraordinary effort, and can cost one's life. I don't think that all of us oath-bound sorcerers essentially sacrificing ourselves would be much of a victory."

"I don't disagree," Rochelle said, "but as we discussed earlier, they may not all be sorcerers."

"Besides, it doesn't take killing someone to beat them," Janna added. "If we make the cost of their victory too high, they may give up."

"Or they may not," Thorne said.

Tir turned to Marlys. "We don't have to plan an entire campaign. We only need to determine our next step."

Marlys leaned back in her chair. "Tir, you said you read books along the spell passage and at the Library of Sorcery about the sorcerous wars."

Tir nodded. "I did."

"I presume the Library has a large collection of accounts of that time." Marlys looked from Genevieve to Blair.

"We do," Blair affirmed.

"That's our first step, then," Marlys said. "Find out what they did and see if there's anything we can make use of."

"There are a lot of books," Blair said. "Serena and I are capable of using the speed-reading spell, but others can't."

"Serena taught me the spell," Nessa said. "I've been practicing. I can use it."

"If you three are willing to go to the Library," Marlys said, "you may be able to gather the information relatively quickly."

"We may not find any strategy we can use even if we read them," Serena said.

"At least we would have tried," Marlys said. "And if we need you back here, you can return almost instantly."

"I'll read," Blair said.

"I'll go," Nessa said.

"I'm willing to read," Serena said, "but even though I can return quickly, I am uneasy about leaving. If there's a surprise attack, seconds would count."

Marlys nodded. "We will have to remain on alert. We will need to have groups of sorcerers on watch day and night, say, in three shifts. That way one-third will be sleeping at any one time. Those on duty would contact the other regions frequently to find out if there's any activity we need to respond to."

"And investigate if any region becomes silent," Rochelle said.

"Yes." Marlys stood and looked around the room. "Are there volunteers for watch duty?"

Every sorcerer's hand went up.

Marlys sat again. "Celestine, can you organize the groups?"

"I'd be happy to."

Oriana spoke up. "What of us apprentices? We want to help."

Marlys heard sounds of assent.

Celestine raised her head. "You can observe and learn. We can still have lessons. The fortress still needs cooks and cleaners and errand-runners. Those are vital tasks, even if it does not seem so."

"Speaking of remaining alert," Voni said, "those of us not living at the fortress need to get back home. We have to protect our local areas and we can respond faster if we're closer."

"Of course," Marlys said.

Voni stood and motioned to the Valleyview sorcerers and apprentices to gather. Others took that as a signal to bring their households together as well. Everyone rose to their feet.

"I'll send instructions for watch groups through the sorcerous channels for those leaving now," Celestine said.

As the sorcerers began to depart, the hall began to feel empty. The remaining sorcerers clustered near Marlys's table. "Janna," called Marlys as Janna turned to go, "would you be willing to leave us your prize? We'll return it."

Janna stepped to Marlys and handed the pin to her. "Study it all you want. I can always get another," she added with a grin.

Elspeth stepped next to her and put a hand gently on Janna's back. "Come, we need to retrieve our formal clothes and go." Elspeth turned to Marlys briefly and raised an eyebrow, shaking her head slightly.

Marlys smiled and nodded in response.

When only the Goldenvalley assembly, plus Genevieve and Blair, remained in the hall, Marlys spoke up. "There's one more task we can accomplish promptly."

"Which is?" Tir asked.

"We, or at least I, need to go to Overlook and inspect the sorcerous weapons there. Kayli told us that they were to activate in time of need. Let's see if they'll come to life now."

Tir chuckled. "Let's hope the weapons sense our need."

"That's what I intend to find out," Marlys said. "Tir, I'll take the spelled arrow you drew out of Blair's back along with Janna's pin. That might convince the weapons to cooperate."

"You speak of those weapons as if they can think," Thorne said.

"Not think," Genevieve said, "but possibly those who constructed the weapons spelled them to speak words given to them. We have such artifacts in the Library District."

"That's an idea," Marlys said. "Can you check the ones that you have to see if they'll respond?"

Genevieve nodded. "Of course. I regret not contributing more to your deliberations. I'm still feeling weary from the injury, and am remiss in not thanking you for healing me earlier."

"I was glad to do it," Marlys said, "and I understand that you're still recovering."

Blair stood and nodded in Tir's direction. "And I thank you again for healing me." Blair picked up his bloody shirt and faced Genevieve. "I'll cast the spell to take us home."

"I'll go with you," Nessa said.

"I'll ask to be excused, at least for now," Serena said. "But don't hesitate to call if you think I can be of service."

"I think Nessa and I can get a good start," Blair said. "You can count on us to contact you swiftly if we need you."

Genevieve slowly rose to her feet. Blair extended a hand to steady her.

"May the Bright Beings watch over you," Marlys said in farewell.

"And with you," Genevieve said.

Nessa put an arm around Genevieve's waist as Blair cast the transportation spell. All three stepped into it.

When they were gone, Tir slid the arrow over the table toward Marlys. "Here's the arrow. I cleaned the blood from it. I can still feel that it's spelled."

Marlys took the arrow.

"I hope I can go with you to Overlook," Tir said.

"I want to go," Serena said.

"I know weapons," Rochelle said, "I'll go, too."

Marlys turned to Zaria. "That will leave Zaria as the only Librarian in Goldenvalley while we're gone."

Astrid walked over and sat. "I just talked to Briarhill. Everything's quiet."

"We gave them quite a thrashing despite our sorcerous limits," Rochelle said, "and if they're not all sorcerers, they're going to be busy tending their wounds."

"No doubt planning their next attack," Zaria said. "But go to Overlook. All four of you. It's important. We can contact you quickly if the need arises."

"I'm not planning to leave until after breakfast tomorrow," Marlys said. "It's been a long evening, and I want to have a clear, rested head to examine those artifacts."

"We all need that," Serena said.

Celestine returned to the group. Sitting with them, she said, "I've assigned the Goldenvalley watches. The sorcerer-trainers at the other centers have told me that they will take on the task of assigning watches in their areas. We're as prepared as we can be at this point."

"Thank you," Marlys said.

"I agree that we must take all the rest we can, whenever we can," Thorne said. "I don't doubt that our opponents will do everything they can to exhaust us."

Chapter 4

The next morning, Astrid had nearly finished her meal by the time Marlys and the others entered the dining hall for breakfast.

"I took the overnight watch," she said as Marlys sat down with a tray. "Briarhill still reports nothing. The sorcerous channels are ablaze with activity. Everyone is checking in with each other. The entire continent is on alert. But no one detects any threats at the moment."

"Thank you," Marlys said. "May the Bright Beings watch over your sleep."

Astrid stood and made a move to take her plates, but Oriana breezed in, and with a smile, removed Astrid's plates and utensils and waved Astrid away. Astrid nodded her appreciation and slowly strolled out.

Marlys turned to her dining companions as she reached for a cup of tea.

"I had a thought," Tir said as he buttered a bread roll. "What are we going to tell the citizenry?"

"Even without sorcerous channels," Rochelle said, "word will spread from the usual travelers going from here to there, just not as quickly. After all, the raid on Riverglen was only what, two days ago?"

"At least at first," Serena said, "the citizens probably will have the same reaction as they did when we dealt with the volcanic ash: confidence that the sorcerers will take care of it."

"I only hope we can meet their expectations," Marlys said.

After breakfast, Marlys, Serena, Tir, and Rochelle appeared at Overlook. They emerged from the transportation spell next to the tower, where Kayli waited for them.

"The legends say that these weapons will come alive when there is a need," Kayli said. "How can they tell if there's a need?"

Tir raised the spelled arrow, clutched in his hand. "An arrow that can penetrate a sorcerer's defensive spells should demonstrate a need."

"We hope," Rochelle said.

Using the climbing spell, they reached the top of the tower. Kayli opened the door. Marlys, holding the pin Janna gave her, and Tir, holding the arrow, stepped in first.

Before anyone could cast an illuminating spell, the room lit up brilliantly. Marlys heard a sound like dozens of tiny bells chiming at once.

"I've never seen or heard that before," Kayli said.

Rochelle scanned the room. "The artifacts are glowing."

Only one piece of furniture graced the circular room: a table, also circular, in the middle. Marlys remembered examining the artifacts on that table when they first traversed the spell passage. As she strolled around, pin in hand, she heard a voice.

"A charm to deflect simple magic," the voice said. "Solution: if stronger spells cannot be cast, use this to overwhelm the charm."

Marlys turned in the direction of the voice. It seemed to have originated from one of the artifacts on the wall.

"A man's voice," Tir said.

"Perhaps of a sorcerer expert in creating charms?" Rochelle said.

From elsewhere in the room, another voice sounded. "The creation of a charm is a demanding task, only possible among sorcerers of exceptional skill and strength. The making of perilous sorcerous armaments requires an even higher level of proficiency, ingenuity, and sacrifice, and few can attain it. These are such artifacts. Use them cautiously and well, for none alive have the power to duplicate or replace them."

They all remained still, silent, listening for more.

When they heard nothing else, Kayli said, "That voice was different. It echoed."

"A Bright Being?" Rochelle ventured.

"What few records of Bright Beings speaking are ancient," Serena said. "I read a handful of pages of such conversations in the Library. What they said is that Bright Beings' speech reminds one of a song."

Tir shrugged. "Who can tell?"

"It is possible to spell an object to talk," Marlys said. "As we just heard, it is difficult, and not commonly done. I've tried it, just for the experience. The voice that came back to me, however, was not my own. I don't think one can control how it sounds."

"So we have no way of knowing who or what provided these voices," Tir said.

"That would be my guess," Serena said.

Marlys exhaled slowly. "In any event, we need to concentrate on our task." She reached for an object on the wall and drew it toward her. "This vibrated and brightened when it identified the pin."

Rochelle leaned over and scrutinized it. "It looks like a vambrace."

Marlys opened it and placed it on her forearm.

Rochelle gasped. "Are you sure it's safe to do that?"

Marlys tilted her head. "I more or less received permission. It fits well. It's not burning or painful."

"If we're in dire need," Tir said, "and we are, we're supposed to be able to use these. They should be safe for us to handle." Slowly, he started to walk around the table, holding up the arrow.

"Use this for protection against spells and spelled weapons," came a voice from the wall.

Tir leaned over to examine the artifact. He lifted it from a hook. "Chest protector." After placing the arrow on the circular table, he strapped it on. "It molds to my body."

Serena moved around Tir to scrutinize the next object on the wall. "It seems that there was some sort of concealing spell in effect when we were here earlier. Before, we couldn't even guess what these were used for. Now they look different. The uses seem clearer upon inspection."

"This will increase physical strength," a voice said.

"I'll take that," Serena said, removing it from its hook. "It's a belt." She buckled it around her waist.

"Let's see what they have for me," Rochelle said, proceeding to another wall section.

"Take this. Point it at an opponent to tell whether the opponent is a sorcerer," said a voice.

Rochelle removed an artifact shaped like a javelin. "Now this is something I need."

Marlys turned to Kayli. "Do you wish to see if something responds to you?"

Kayli shook her head and smiled. "No, I'm the host here. I'm content to observe as you explore."

"You might find something to defend Overlook if necessary," Tir said.

"Overlook has its own defenses," Kayli said. "The glowing orbs nullify the casting of spells if more than one sorcerer is present. The fortress is already spelled against conventional attack."

The others continued their search. The artifacts continued to speak out. They gathered objects to increase the energy of a defender, decrease the energy of an attacker, cause an opponent to flee in terror, move someone from one location to another, and weaken limbs. They also took the glass they had tested on their earlier visit, which explained that it was for telling whether someone was being deceitful.

"What does it mean when it says 'linking weapon?'" Tir asked as Rochelle picked up an artifact shaped like a lance.

"No idea." Rochelle faced the weapon. "Can you say more?"

The weapon remained silent.

"Apparently not," Marlys said.

"They don't answer questions, it seems," Tir said.

"I'm taking it anyway," Rochelle said. "We'll probably find out."

"We'll have to," Serena said. "We don't know how strong their actions are, we don't know whether they work on one individual at a time or a group all at once, we don't know whether they're directional, and we don't know if they have a distance limit. And we won't know until we start using them."

"Sounds risky," Kayli said.

"Riskier to be without them," Rochelle said. "We could have used these in our earlier melee."

Serena approached the last unexplored section of the wall and waved her hand over the objects there. "No response from these."

"Maybe they're no longer capable of working?" Tir said.

Serena turned to him. "I doubt it. Magic doesn't expire. A spell can be canceled, or have built-in time limits, but it's not like a candle that goes out when the wick reaches its end."

"That's the truth," Kayli said. "We have magical objects in the Spell Passage which seem to have existed since the dawn of time."

Marlys turned to Kayli. "Do you mind if we add them to what we already have, in case they come to life later or we can determine how they work?"

"You need them more than I do," Kayli said. "Take them."

"...and hope they don't turn on us," Tir said.

"I think somehow they can tell that we're aligned with the purposes of their makers," Marlys said. "I'm willing to chance it."

"We'll exercise caution," Serena said. "That's all we can do with any of these."

"How can we take all of these home?" Rochelle asked.

Kayli indicated a shelf behind her. "I suspect that's what all these bags and boxes are for. All the station hosts here have presumed those are the containers they arrived in, long ago."

Marlys and the others returned to Goldenvalley to see Genevieve, Blair, and Nessa in the audience room, surrounded by apprentices and other sorcerers.

"We just arrived," Blair explained.

As Marlys, Tir, Serena, and Rochelle put their packs on the floor, Nessa leaned forward. "Did you bring the trapping artifact?"

"Trapping artifact?" Serena asked.

Nessa began to search the bags and boxes. "It looks like trident...here it is." She plucked it out and held it up. "It creates a sorcerous perimeter around a group that they can't get out of."

"There were several artifacts that didn't identify themselves," Marlys said. "We just brought them with us. That was one of them."

"How did you know about these?" Serena asked. "Did you find a book with a list of weapons and descriptions?"

Blair held up a book. "Not directly. But in the records of the battles, the writers said things such as, 'We corralled our opponents using the trapping trident and rendered them harmless with the paralysis weapon,' or "We decimated an entire company using the attacking mace.'"

Genevieve stepped closer to the packs. "What were you able to bring?"

Marlys and Serena explained the use of everything they could identify.

"Any idea about what's left over?" Tir asked.

"No, but we may find descriptions of these in other books," Nessa said.

"Did the books explain why some of these artifacts talk and others don't?" Serena asked.

"Apparently it depends on the sorcerer who crafted them," Genevieve said. "Some sorcerers spelled the objects to explain themselves. Other sorcerers simply told their colleagues how the weapon was used."

"We heard a voice saying that none alive could make more weapons like these," Serena said.

Genevieve nodded. "It's beyond the powers of even you and Marlys and me. The records state that in order to spell these objects, sorcerers would draw on the energy of the universe itself as well as their own sorcerous strength. The result was that after the weapon had been fashioned, the makers lost the ability to cast spells, even household spells, for the rest of their lives."

"Did the books say how they were able to draw on the powers of the universe?" Serena asked.

"No," Blair said, "but they did say that all records of the technique were destroyed, and those utilizing this magic bound themselves with an oath never to reveal it. When they died, the knowledge of the spell died with them."

"They felt that an opponent might discover the spell and use it against them," Nessa said.

"Very wise," Thorne said, "but we can't accomplish anything by discussing this further. We have to concentrate on what we do with what we have now."

"Agreed," Marlys said.

Rochelle lifted the javelin. "I want to see how this works. This alone will help immensely."

"What is it?" Celestine asked.

"Supposedly," Rochelle said. "It will reveal who is a sorcerer and who isn't."

"Very useful," Zaria observed.

"Mind if I point it at you?" Rochelle asked.

"Go ahead," Zaria said.

Rochelle pointed the javelin.

Marlys saw a blue leaf outline on Zaria's forehead.

Rochelle looked around. "Do you all see it? The blue leaf?"

"Yes, on her arm," Tir said.

"No, on her forehead," Marlys said.

When others claimed to see the leaf image elsewhere, Rochelle moved her head. "When I look at her feet, it's on her feet. When I look at her waist, it's on her waist."

"Oh, now I see how it works," Tir said.

"How long does it last?" Thorne asked.

"I guess we'll find out," Tir said.

"Let me try it on an apprentice," Rochelle said. "Oriana, are you willing?"

Oriana grinned and stepped forward.

Rochelle pointed the javelin at her.

"I see a red bird," Thorne said.

Rochelle moved her head again. "It works the same way. I see a red bird on her everywhere I look."

Marlys saw Serena examining a stack on the floor near Nessa.

"What did you bring, other than a book?" Serena asked.

"Protective spells." Genevieve lifted an item that appeared to be a large stake. "You know that the Library District is walled off magically from the rest of the continent by spells cast centuries ago."

"And reinforced lately by further boundary spells," Blair added.

Serena nodded. "But I never came across any writings explaining how those spells are cast."

"You won't," Genevieve said. "We pass those from generation to generation orally. Some of the older spells have been lost in time." Genevieve held up the stake. "But this can create a perimeter just about as strong."

"We have spells here to protect a town or a farmstead," Thorne said. "They're quite effective."

"No, Aunt Thorne," Nessa said. "Our spells can prevent entry or exit by animals or citizens. They can also deflect weaker spells. They won't stop a stronger sorcerer such as Argent, and they'll fail against other sorcerous weapons." She picked up another stake. "This, plunged into the ground, will surround an area that a sorcerer designates so that nothing goes in or out except at the will of someone within the perimeter when the spell is cast. The stake can then be removed and used again in another location."

Blair held up the book. "It's all described in there. Another interesting item: the sorcerous wars ended when the surviving aggressors were cast into the island worlds. They had their sorcerous weapons with them."

Thorne snorted. "They weren't disarmed first?"

"No time," Blair said. "It was critical to get them out of the way at once. When cornered at last, they shouted they would end their lives and the lives of all who had opposed them rather than surrender."

"We don't yet know how they might have carried through their threat," Nessa said, "but it was clear that the Librarians confronting them took them seriously and had to act immediately to save themselves."

"That at least explains how Argent was able to get sorcerous weapons," Thorne said.

Lyra ran into the room. "Edwina says the rogues are back and Briarhill needs help."

Chapter 5

"We need to arm ourselves and go," Marlys said, taking the vambrace and putting it on.

"You're going now even though you haven't thoroughly tested the weapons?" Thorne said, aghast.

"We're better prepared than we were last time." Serena began to sort through the packs on the floor. "According to the voice, sorcerous weapons and stronger spells will defeat their charmed defenses."

"I can mark everyone right away," Rochelle said, brandishing the javelin, "and then we'll know who we're dealing with. If they're not sorcerers, use a more powerful attacking spell than the knockout one."

"I'll take the terror hammer." Tir removed it from the pack.

"I'm ready." Zaria twirled a baton. "This will cause my opponent to tire, if I understand your description correctly."

Blair reached into a pack and brought out a metallic shaft with a head shaped like an elongated disk. "I'll take the one that increases one's energy. I can use it on myself or anyone else who seems to be tiring."

Thorne sighed. "If you're determined to go, I'll go, too. "But I think the bludgeon you found that can cause someone's limbs to weaken will help even more, especially since it seems all I have to do is point it at someone."

"Most of these work by pointing." Serena grabbed the trident.

Marlys took the hook. "Then let's go to where we're needed." She cast the transportation spell.

Those who had armed themselves gathered together and walked through to Riverglen. Marlys saw the Briarhill sorcerers trying in vain to push back the attackers with defensive spells. The men continued to advance. Argent led the way, demolishing the protective spells the Briarhill sorcerers had cast, leaving them vulnerable to his forces.

Rochelle immediately pointed the javelin at the attackers, quickly marking each individual with the spell. Argent and all of his fighters had their backs to the Goldenvalley sorcerers, and had not spotted the sorcerers in their rush toward Riverglen.

Thorne, Zaria, and Serena surged forward first, assaulting the fighters with red-bird markings using spells and sorcerous weapons.

Argent sensed his new opponents and turned. "Look to your rear!" he shouted.

"I want to use the terror hammer," Tir said, "but I need an angle where I won't be affecting the Briarhill people as well."

Serena used the trident to create a perimeter around the main group of Argent's men, separating them from the Briarhill sorcerers.

Tir aimed the terror hammer at Argent's men with a sweeping motion. Men screamed and ran headlong toward the woods, but collided with Serena's barrier, which yielded a little with their momentum, but held.

This left a smaller group around Argent that the Goldenvalley sorcerers threw blocking spells at.

Meanwhile, Thorne plowed through straight to Argent. She pointed the bludgeon right and left, keeping the attackers from reaching her. Her face showed grim determination.

Argent spotted her closing the gap. Seeing her and the other sorcerers rushing toward him, raising their own weapons, he opened a portal to the island worlds. The maelstrom sucked his men inside. Argent then stepped through the portal himself and closed it.

The sorcerers had all anchored themselves when the portal opened to keep from being pulled through.

Once the tumult subsided, Rochelle said, "There was only one sorcerer: Argent."

"That doesn't mean he might not have sorcerer allies elsewhere," Thorne said.

"I agree," Genevieve said. "We all have to be on our guard."

Edwina and other Briarhill sorcerers hurried to Marlys. "Thank you, and how did you do that?"

Rochelle hefted the javelin. "We have sorcerous weapons now."

Genevieve held up one of the stakes she had brought from the Library. "I'm going to show you how to wall off your town sorcerously with this. Then I'll give this stake to you so that you can do the same throughout your region. That will prevent this Argent and his forces from razing your settlements."

"We set a protective spell, but as you saw, it didn't work," Edwina said.

"This will," Genevieve said. "Once the sorcerous barrier is set, no human or animal can go in or out except at the action of someone inside the boundary at the time it was set up."

"That would mean we would need a guardian at the roads going in and out of town at all times," Edwina said.

Genevieve nodded. "But it does not necessarily have to be a sorcerer. Choose people of good character that you can trust. I'll explain everything and I'll be sure you know how to use it before I leave."

"There may be some grumbling," Edwina said. "Citizens are used to going in and out at any point at will. But if it protects everyone from being attacked, I think all will go along with it."

"Once we defeat this Argent," Genevieve said, "you can cancel the spell, if you wish."

Edwina nodded. "That will also help. But what about going in and out of a protected area using an end point spell?"

"The sorcerers who designed the stakes seemed to have had that in mind," Genevieve said. "As long as we're inside the barrier when it is set, we can go in and out using magic."

Once the protective spell was in place at Riverglen, Marlys and the others returned to Goldenvalley.

"How did it go?" Celestine asked as they emerged in the audience room.

"No injuries among us," Marlys said. "Tir set most of them running in terror. Argent sent all of his followers through to the island worlds with him."

"He'll be back," Thorne said. "You can count on it."

"Not quickly," Zaria said. "Besides the injuries we inflicted, my guess is it will take time for the terror, fatigue, and weakening spells to fade."

"I can still see a faint red bird image on Oriana," Serena said, "though it's not as clear as it was at first. The spells we used may still be affecting Argent's men, wherever they are."

Genevieve indicated the stakes she had left in the room. "Blair and I, and Nessa, if she's willing, need to get back to the Library. You've seen how the barrier spell is cast. Briarhill has my stake and their sorcerers will carry it from town to town there. Can you do the same here with the other stakes I brought?"

"We can organize a relay," Celestine said. "We can start by sending sorcerers with the stakes to our areas. Each area can then send a sorcerer with a stake to the next area and pass it on for their sorcerers to use and carry elsewhere. When every area is protected, they can bring the stakes back to us."

Marlys nodded. "That should cover the continent quickly."

"I'll take a stake," Zaria said, "and surround the fortress here. Then I'll go to Valleyview and use the stake to cast a protective spell there. They can carry the stakes to other places in their area from there." She hurried out.

Tir picked up a stake. "I'll start at the remote mining area. They can work their way inward."

Genevieve, Blair, and Nessa left after Zaria returned and confirmed that barrier was set around the fortress. Tir and Zaria disappeared into their respective transportation spells soon thereafter.

When they were gone, Marlys turned to the remaining sorcerers and apprentices in the room. "Meanwhile, we still have our regular duties."

"They're being done," Celestine said. "We're still making regular visits to the towns and farmsteads in the vicinity."

"The cows are being milked, the horses groomed, the animals fed, the gardens and orchards tended," Oriana added.

Marlys nodded. "Thank you for all of that."

Serena walked around the artifacts they had left on the floor. "Meanwhile, we need to try these out and see how they work."

"Very carefully try them out to see how they work," Thorne added.

Serena glanced in Thorne's direction. "Of course." She reached for an object which appeared to be a glove. Fitting it on her right hand, she held it up for all to see. "There seems to be a disc embedded in the palm...or something stiff, at least."

"For grasping and crushing?" Rochelle guessed.

Serena turned to Rochelle. "Would you be willing to let me take you by the hand?"

Rochelle pulled on thick fighting gloves. "If you break a bone, I can always heal it."

Marlys watched as Serena carefully wrapped her fingers around Rochelle's hand.

After a few seconds, Rochelle said, "Nothing."

Serena shook her head. "I don't feel anything, either."

"Then what does it do?" Rochelle asked.

"Maybe it's just a glove," Thorne said.

Serena stepped toward the weapons again. "Perhaps it works with another weapon?" She surveyed the weapons, still resting on the floor with the packs, and held her gloved hand over the stack.

Immediately, the mace flew upward and smacked the palm of the glove.

"That was fast!" Rochelle exclaimed.

Serena had not closed her fingers over the mace's shaft.

"Will it stick to the glove?" Marlys asked.

"Let's see." Serena kept her fingers spread.

The mace dropped to the floor with a clang.

"I have an idea." Rochelle held up the javelin. "Serena, raise your gloved hand, palm facing in this direction."

When Serena did so, the javelin flew into her hand. This time, Serena grasped it to keep it from falling.

Rochelle grinned. "That confirms what it does."

Serena pried the javelin loose with her left hand and gave it back to Rochelle. "Yes. It acted when I flexed my fingers, both times. The disk seemed to nudge my hand into action."

"It's good that you have control," Thorne said. "Otherwise we'd have objects flying all around toward you."

Serena carefully removed the glove and placed it in her pants pocket. "For safety." She bent and picked up a lance. "I'm especially curious as to what this tethering weapon does."

"So am I," Marlys said. "Go ahead and point the lance at me and we'll see what happens."

Serena did so.

"I don't feel anything," Marlys said after a few moments.

"Neither do I," Serena said.

"Keep pointing it at me, and I'll move." Marlys started to walk in a circle around Serena. The lance point followed her.

"It's compelling me to move with it," Serena said.

Marlys stopped.

"No, don't stop," Serena said. "I want to see if it has a range."

"Let me walk outside to see if walls will inhibit it." Marlys walked to the nearest exit, opened the door, stepped outside, passed the barrier, and closed it again. She walked toward the barn.

"It's still following her," Serena said.

Marlys turned, thinking Serena had walked behind her, but saw nothing. "Serena?"

"I can hear you even though I'm still inside," Serena said.

"I can hear you, too. I shouldn't be able to, but I can," Marlys said.

"It's not like the sorcerous channels, though," Serena said. "There's sound but no image. I can see you through the windows, but that's all."

"Let's try a longer distance." Marlys cast an end point spell. "I'll head toward Frosthollow." She stepped through, and when she emerged, she could see the fortress in the far distance. "Is it still following me?"

"Yes," Serena's voice said. "I can still hear you clearly, too."

"Let me go to the tower at Overlook." When Marlys stepped out, she saw the Overlook fortress nearby, but Kayli was not outside. "I'm at Overlook."

"I can still hear you," Serena said.

"Let's give it the most difficult test of all." Marlys cast the transportation spell to take her to the Library of Sorcery. When she emerged, she saw Nessa sitting on a stone bench in the garden outside the Library building. An open book was in her lap, and at her left was a stack of books.

She looked up at Marlys. "Did you have a message too secret to talk through the sorcerous channels?"

"No," Marlys said. "Serena and I are testing out the tethering weapon."

"Who are you talking to?" Serena said. "I can hear only you."

"Nessa," Marlys said.

"Are you talking to Serena?" Nessa said. "I can't hear her."

Marlys nodded. "Apparently the one at the other end can only hear the person tethered."

"Can you see Serena?" Nessa asked.

"No, and Serena can't see me. She can only hear me."

Nessa patted the book. "I haven't read about the tethering weapon yet, but I have information on others. Do you have a moment?"

"Serena, can you wait a brief time while I talk to Nessa about weapons?" Marlys said aloud.

"Of course. Just tell me what you learned when you get back."

Marlys sat on Nessa's right. "What have you found?"

Nessa faced her. "Remember the mace weapon?"

"The one that the book said decimated the enemy? Yes."

"I found out what it does. It's a much stronger version of the knockout spell. Point it, make a striking motion, and the person is unconscious. Can't be revived except through sorcery. No sorcery, they're dead within days."

"That's lethal," Marlys said.

"I haven't even reached lethal yet," Nessa said. "Did you see or retrieve a battle axe?"

Marlys shook her head. "No, nothing like that."

"Nothing like that here, either," Nessa said. "Genevieve and the others have searched. We have to hope Argent doesn't have it."

"Why?"

"Point it at someone and it's instant death. Doesn't matter if it's a sorcerer. Doesn't matter if they have a spell of protection, except maybe that chest protector that Tir has. It won't go through the sorcerous barrier that Genevieve showed us how to set up, but those are the only defenses I read about that work against it."

"I appreciate the warning," Marlys said. "Anything else?"

Nessa shook her head. "Nothing that you haven't discovered already. I haven't read anything about the tethering spell either. It's good that you tested it."

Marlys stood. "Thanks. I'll head back to Goldenvalley. Give my regards to the sorcerers here."

"Of course. May the blessings of the Bright Beings light your way home."

When Marlys emerged from the transportation spell, Serena still held the lance. The end still pointed at Marlys.

Serena shook the lance.

"Does that break the connection?" Marlys said.

"I presume so," Serena said. "The weapon itself prompted me to act." She held the weapon, point down, then up, but it did not point it to Marlys again.

"I noticed that with the weapon I had," Thorne said. "Something about it caused me to hold it just so to activate it and hold it another way to stop its action."

"Probably part of the spell, along with the verbal instructions," Rochelle said.

Serena returned the lance to the weapons stack. "What did you learn from Nessa?"

Rochelle suggested that they create an armory, at least a temporary one, at a corner of the audience hall. Since Marlys and other sorcerers and apprentices had carpentry skills, they constructed a place to display and label the weapons quickly. Sorcery sped the process.

Tir returned as they were setting up the display, bringing Durand with him.

Once all exchanged greetings, Durand said, "I wondered if I could help. I'm willing to go and talk to Argent, to see if he can be persuaded to stop his assault."

"Ha!" Thorne crossed her arms in front of her. "He doesn't engage in chat."

"He has said nothing but terse directions to his men to attack when we've seen him," Marlys affirmed.

"Further," Thorne said, "he seems focused on avenging himself on me for throwing him into the island worlds in the first place, and on wreaking as much havoc as he can in the process."

Durand shrugged. "Maybe, but at least you'll have another sorcerer helping you."

"Stay as long as you wish," Marlys said.

Zaria returned soon after Tir and Durand did and approached Marlys. "The protective spells have been set at Valleyview and one of the stakes has been passed according to Celestine's plan. But there's another urgent matter I need to tell you about."

"What is it?" Marlys asked.

"There's been an increase in travel on the roads. People have been leaving Riverglen and the surrounding farmsteads to stay with friends and relatives elsewhere. They don't feel safe after Argent's attacks."

"Everyone?" Tir asked.

"No, we checked with Edwina and she says most people have stayed in Riverglen or come to another nearby town to be protected. But it's more than the usual journeyers going from town to town. Voni and Elspeth said some have stopped at Valleyview briefly on their way to more distant destinations."

"Sorcerers have taken in citizens after disasters before," Thorne said, "but only rarely, and only for a few days until we could arrange for other shelter."

Zaria nodded. "Voni and Elspeth said the only ones lingering are those without family or friends elsewhere, and they're finding residents in the town willing to take them in." Zaria turned to Marlys. "Among the ones lingering at Valleyview were Caleb, Jessie, and their toddler."

"Did something happen?" Marlys said.

Zaria nodded. "Celeb was out in the field a few days ago. He saw a large group of men coming. Afraid that they were bandits, he and Jessie and the little one took refuge in the storm cellar. He said they were there for quite some time, with a lot of noise above them. When all had been quiet for a long time, they ventured out. The men were gone, but the farmstead had been stripped of just about anything edible. Some animals fled, others taken. He went to Valleyview for shelter."

"That explains how Argent and his men are getting supplies," Thorne said.

Realization struck Marlys like a thunderbolt. "They've come to Goldenvalley!"

Chapter 6

"Marlys," Esme said, "I have family near Valleyview. I need to check on them."

Others in the room added similar requests.

Marlys nodded. "By all means. Whenever you're ready, use the end point spell to go to your relatives. Come back here when they're safe."

"What about us apprentices?" Oriana asked.

"We'll pair you with a sorcerer to take you," Celestine said.

"Since this Argent is after Thorne," Durand said, "I would expect him to come here to confront her."

Thorne lifted an eyebrow. "I sent him to the island worlds while I was standing in the Briarhill region. Riverglen is in the southeast corner of that region. He should not be able to connect me with this location."

"He would not have to go far from Riverglen to reach this area. Valleyview is in the southwest corner of Goldenvalley," Marlys said. "That's the reason I went to Valleyview for my sorcerer training. It was closer than a Briarhill training center."

A group of sorcerers and apprentices left the dining hall quickly.

Durand lingered in the room, finishing his tea. "No family here, Marlys?"

Marlys shook her head. "My parents retired to Swangate, near your home."

Durand nodded. "I know the area."

"My brother is a magistrate in Cloverdell," Marlys added.

"It's good that the rest of us here have relatives far away," Rochelle said.

"Or none at all," Thorne observed. "Many sorcerers and apprentices I've known have had no family to speak of."

"Distance might not protect them, if Argent is able to build his forces," Durand said.

"That is the reason we need to defeat him as soon as we can," Thorne said.

"Yes, particularly since we now know he may have access to even more deadly weapons," Marlys said. "Nessa found at the Library that at the end of the sorcerous wars, those sent to the island worlds still had their weapons with them. Argent could well have found those weapons."

"What sort of weapons?" Durand asked.

Marlys stood and motioned to Durand and Zaria to follow. "Let me take you to our new armory and I'll show you what we have here."

After Marlys, Serena, and Rochelle had described the weapons, Marlys turned to Zaria. "You're still spending part of the evening on the sorcerous channels teaching spells we learned at the Library?"

"Most nights, yes," Zaria said.

"Tonight, spread the word about what we learned about the weapons today." Marlys said.

"I will," Zaria said when Marlys finished. "The others have to know about this."

"We especially have to make a plan about what to do if we see Argent with the killer battle axe Nessa told you about," Thorne said.

"I agree," Marlys said.

"Soon," Thorne said. "He could show up at any time."

"Since we realized that Zaria had the power to attack sorcerers," Rochelle said, "she and I have been going over strategies to use if we ever needed to restrain a fellow sorcerer. I have been drawing on my training as a magistrate's deputy as to what to do in the case of a kidnapping, for instance."

"I don't think that will help us against Argent," Thorne said.

"Coercion takes many forms," Rochelle said.

Zaria nodded toward Serena. "We've consulted Serena on various offensive and defensive spells to use."

"They don't seem to have helped us so far," Thorne said.

"I disagree," Serena said. "We're all still alive so far."

"Very well," Thorne said. "What is your plan if he has the battle axe?"

"Use the stake and throw a sorcerous barrier around us," Serena said. "Someone can put on the protective chest piece, walk around the barrier, and then use the glove to wrench it away from him."

"If Argent has his forces with him, we'd have to protect our champion from them," Rochelle said.

"That would mean leaving the barrier," Marlys said.

"If the plan works as I describe," Serena said, "the champion would have the battle axe within moments."

"Plans can go astray, and often do," Thorne said.

Serena turned to Thorne. "They do. But this, at least, gives us a start to build upon. What's your plan?"

"Time-freeze him and take the weapon away," Thorne said.

"That worked once, probably when he was not expecting to see any sorcerers," Rochelle said. "He may have spells preventing that now."

"The time-freeze spell doesn't work on those with that pin Jana gave us," Tir said. "I've tried it, and so have others here. I don't remember him wearing one when we first saw him, but he probably wears one now."

Durand gestured toward the armory. "The corralling weapon might be used to keep him in a circle so tight he can't move. I doubt the weapon could be used if he just holds it, or there would be a lot of unintended deaths, including his if he accidentally pointed it at himself."

"Could work," Rochelle said.

A silence followed. Marlys said, "I'm sure other ideas will occur to us as we think about this. Meanwhile, we have our usual tasks, as well as awaiting the return of our sorcerers and apprentices checking on family."

By mid-afternoon, everyone except Esme had returned.

Marlys strolled around the fortress, watching for Esme to return. Her end point spell could cause her to appear anywhere in the fortress, though the audience room and dining hall were the roomiest places.

Wondering if Esme might reappear outside, Marlys made her way to the main entrance. She stood at the open doorway, looking around and down the road. The weather was sunny and warm, with a slight breeze. Marlys took the opportunity to check the area around the fortress, watching their animals graze, noting the ripening fruit on the trees, seeing people traveling each way on the main road.

Presently, Marlys became aware of a horse cart on the road heading west. Instead of passing the intersection between the road and the path to the fortress, the driver guided the cart up the hill. As they came closer, Marlys saw a man driving, a woman holding an infant, and a toddler sitting between the two adults.

The man stopped the cart maybe ten paces away from the front steps and helped the others off. He walked directly to Marlys, stopping at the edge of the barrier near the front steps.

He took his cap off and bowed. "Please, esteemed sorcerer, my family needs shelter. Raiders came to our farmstead and took everything. We barely made it out alive. We know of no one else to turn to, no where else to go. I can find work in the next town, maybe, but please take my wife and children."

Marlys had cast a truth spell, and found the account accurate. She opened the barrier. "Of course you can come in. Tie your animal on the post over there by the water trough and stack of hay."

He did so while the woman, carrying the infant in one arm and holding on to the toddler's hand, walked in Marlys's direction.

"You can stay here, too," Marlys called to the man. "We have plenty of empty rooms here and can find one for all of you."

The man bowed to Marlys again.

"What are your names?" Marlys asked. "I'm Marlys, the High Sorcerer here."

"I'm Stavros," the man said. "My wife, Lena, my son, Avril, and the baby is Prima."

"You are welcome," Marlys said, and led them inside. She spotted Lyra in the front hall. "Lyra, will you watch for Esme and let me know when she comes?"

Lyra nodded and walked off.

Marlys paused in her steps and faced the newcomers. "We have guest rooms made up. I'll find one for you."

Going to the rooms required crossing the audience hall, where Thorne and others had gathered at the armory. The guests glanced in that direction. The baby started to cry.

Marlys stopped and peered at the blanket-wrapped infant.

"She's teething," Lena said.

Thorne appeared at their side. "Oh, let me take the little button." She held out her arms. "I've healed many a teething child."

Lena looked from Marlys to Thorne, and slowly handed over the infant.

Thorne took Prima in her arms and smiled. "Don't worry, little button. Your Auntie Thorne knows what do to." She caressed the baby's jaw with her finger. The child quieted. "There. All better now." She handed the infant back to Lena.

Lena nodded. "Thank you, esteemed sorcerer."

Thorne smiled. "My pleasure."

Astrid walked toward them from the bedroom area, apparently just getting up from her day's sleep.

"Astrid, we have guests," Marlys said. "Can you show them to one of our larger rooms?"

"Of course," Astrid said, and escorted them away.

As Marlys and Thorne moved to return to the group at the armory, Lyra ran in, breathless.

"Marlys! Argent is here! He has Esme and is calling for Thorne!

"I'll take care of him!" Thorne said.

Rochelle grabbed her by the upper arm. "No, you don't. We don't give in to hostage-takers. He's not to even see you."

Thorne grimaced. She passed a hand over her face. "There! Good enough?"

Marlys checked out the disguise. Thorne had cast a spell to change her features, and was unrecognizable.

Still holding Thorne's arm, Rochelle said, "Very well, but you are not going out there, and you are not to speak to him. Period."

Thorne wrenched away. "I'll stay here and not call out. For now."

Meanwhile, Serena had buckled the strength belt around her waist. "Zaria, take the spelled arrow and Rochelle's crossbow. Use the end point spell to get behind him. I'll distract him. Shoot him in the back."

"Kill him if you can," Thorne said.

"Does he have a protective spell surrounding him?" Marlys asked.

Serena leaned to one side and looked out the window. "If he does, I'll be able to detect it and cancel it once I'm out beyond the barrier."

"He probably doesn't know how to cast a protective spell," Thorne said. "Or was too careless and confident to cast one."

Zaria grabbed the arrow and crossbow. "There's no sorcery in the world that will direct an arrow, so I can't guarantee where the arrow will strike. I'll do my best."

"All you need to do is hit him." Serena pulled out the tethering pointer and handed it to Tir. "Tether him. Don't let go. And remember not to talk or he'll hear you."

Tir nodded solemnly.

"Thorne! Thorne! Come out!"

Durand looked up and around. "He's amplifying his voice."

Celestine and the apprentices came out of the classroom looking bewildered.

"What is that?" Celestine asked.

Marlys held out an arm toward them. "You can watch, but stay back."

Rochelle peered through the windows. "He's coming around to this side, dragging Esme with him."

Serena joined her in looking out as she strapped on the chest protector. "No killer weapon I can see, but he has a copy of the fatigue-inducing baton strapped on his side. Probably that's how he's kept Esme under control. She looks dazed."

"I think the knife at her throat is doing a thorough job of that," Durand said.

"Let's hope it's not spelled," Thorne said.

Serena turned to Zaria. "Are you ready?"

"Yes, I'll go elsewhere to cast the end point spell so he won't see me do it." Zaria hurried away.

Serena stalked to the side door, sorcerously opened the barrier, stepped through, and just as quickly closed it. She charged straight toward Argent.

Argent spotted her and laughed out loud. "What is this? You're sending a gnat to challenge me? Where's Thorne? Give me Thorne or I'll...."

Thwack! An arrow protruded through Argent's right shoulder. He dropped the knife and let go of Esme. Serena caught her before she fell to the ground, picked her up, and stomped back to the fortress carrying her.

Argent, gurgling with pain and rage, cast spells to heal himself while also attempting to pull out the arrow.

Inside, Durand turned to Tir. "Do you have him?"

Tir, pointing the tethering weapon straight at Argent, nodded grimly.

Serena reached the door. Marlys opened it. Lyra and Rochelle took Esme and helped her inside. Apprentices already had hauled a couch into the room and produced blankets. They set Esme there. Marlys sat beside her.

"Rochelle," Serena said, unbuckling the chest protector, "hand me the pole with the disk. We need to strengthen Esme."

Durand reached over to Serena. "Give me the chest protector." She handed it to him. He strapped it on.

"You aren't going out there?" Thorne said. "I told you, he isn't interested in talking."

"We'll see," Durand said.

Meanwhile, Serena pointed the disk at Esme. Esme came to life, sat up, embraced Marlys, and wept on her shoulder.

"I'm sorry, Marlys, I'm so sorry."

"None of this is your fault."

"But it is," she sobbed.

Marlys gestured at Oriana. "Get some cider or tea for Esme." Oriana hurried to the kitchen.

Durand adjusted the chest protector and looked out the window.

"He's having a time removing the arrow," Rochelle said.

"I'm waiting until he can give me his full attention." Durand walked toward the armory and picked up the glove.

Zaria appeared with crossbow. "I did what I could."

"You did just fine," Rochelle said.

Oriana came back with a mug of hot spiced cider. Esme pulled away from Marlys and took the mug with a shaking hand. She took one sip, swallowed, then took another.

Rochelle knelt on the floor next to the couch and looked up at Esme, who had bowed her head.

"Esme," Rochelle said gently, "we need to know what happened. Anything you can remember can help us defeat Argent."

"I cast an end point and arrived at a wooded area overlooking my family's farmstead. Argent's men were already looting it. I crept a little closer, trying to see if my family was there, when I ran into Stavros and his family. They work on the farm. They told me my family had gone days ago to visit relatives and left him to tend to things. When they saw the raiders coming, they hid in the forest. I said I would help them get away, but before I could cast a spell, Argent grabbed me. He used that weakening bludgeon. I couldn't even speak. He demanded that Stavros tell him where Thorne was or he would kill his wife and children. He said Thorne was at the fortress of Goldenvalley, everyone knew that. He told Stavros to go there and he would follow with me." She began to weep again.

Marlys reached out and put a hand on Esme's shoulder. "None of this was your fault."

Rochelle looked up at Marlys. "If anything, it's our fault for not anticipating something like this. We should have sent out sorcerers in pairs, with weapons."

"How could we know?" Lyra said. "He's never done this before, never got this close before."

Rochelle stood and raised an eyebrow. "It's our job to protect the region. It's our responsibility to anticipate problems."

"We can't foresee every possibility, even when we try," Marlys said.

"Oh, look!" Thorne mocked. "He's figured out how to remove the arrow."

"It's spelled as well as barbed," Rochelle said.

Durand squared his shoulders. "He's finishing healing himself and cleaning the blood from his clothes. I'm going out there."

"Be careful," Marlys said.

Durand smiled and straightened the chest protector. "I always am."

"May the Bright Beings go with you," Marlys said.

Durand grinned. "They always do."

Chapter 7

Outside, Argent shook the bloody arrow in front of him and bellowed, "You'll pay for this! I'll kill you all! I'll burn your houses, your barns, your fields!" He cast a spell toward the fortress. The sorcerous barrier rumbled, but held.

"He throws quite a tantrum, doesn't he?" Celestine said.

"He can't really do that, can he?" Oriana said nervously.

Thorne turned to her. "Don't worry about it, child. He can try, but we can stop him."

Durand stepped outside through the opening in the barrier that Zaria made for him and immediately closed once he was through. Argent turned toward Durand and cast another spell. Durand swayed slightly but continued to stroll toward him, undaunted.

Argent searched the ground for his dropped knife and picked it up. Durand raised his gloved hand. The knife soared straight to Durand's palm, hilt first.

Argent scowled at Durand. "Who are you?" he growled.

"I'm a sorcerer, as you are." Durand said calmly, lowering his hand and inserting the knife in a vest pocket. "My name is Durand."

"Are you here to join me, or thwart me?"

"That depends," Durand said. "What are you offering me?"

"Power," Argent said. "When I conquer this continent, you can rule over a region."

"Why would I do that?" Durand asked.

"Because we are superior," Argent said. "We were designed to rule. We were destined to rule. Ordinary people are incompetent, lazy, bickering fools. They need a strong hand."

"I disagree," Durand said

"Ha!" Argent scoffed.

"It would be exhausting to manage an entire continent," Durand said. "Why not just set up an estate, find those willing to work for you, and manage your manor house?"

He pounded his chest. "I am not going to oversee a mere fiefdom. I was made to order the world. No one could do better than I. With all that I have at my disposal, I will prevail!"

Durand lifted an eyebrow. "You won't succeed here. There's an entire continent of sorcerers opposing you. Not to mention the Library of Sorcery."

"The what?" Argent said.

"The center of sorcery on this world."

"I've never heard of such a place. You're making that up to unsettle me. I will not be taken in by your idle tales!"

"On the contrary, it's very real. Two of the most powerful sorcerers of this era stand in the fortress right behind me."

"Then why are those sorcerers not in front of me instead of you?"

"Perhaps because they cannot be bothered with a petty ruffian."

Argent laughed derisively. "Perhaps because they don't exist!"

"If you continue your campaign, you will find out they very much exist. You will never see them coming."

"Bah!" Argent glared at Durand. "Stop wasting my time. Either join me or get out of my way."

"I will do neither," Durand said.

"Then I will be gone! Beware my return! Join me or bow down before me!" Argent opened a portal to the island worlds.

Durand rooted himself to the ground until the portal closed. He sighed deeply and walked back to the fortress. Zaria again opened the barrier for him.

Once inside, he removed the glove and chest protector and returned them to the armory. "At least we know a little more about his intentions."

"You got more words out of him than I ever did," Thorne said.

Durand lifted an eyebrow. "I had the feeling that he would be more willing to talk to a man, and Tir was occupied."

Meanwhile, Tir struggled with the pointer as if it were a fishing rod which had caught an enormous fish. Serena, recognizing Tir's struggle, sprang into action. She found the disk that increased one's stamina and aimed it at Tir. His grip held.

"You still have a connection in the island worlds?" Thorne asked.

Tir nodded.

Marlys touched Thorne's shoulder. "Tir can't talk to us, Thorne. Argent would hear him. Argent can't hear us, though."

"Oh, yes," Thorne said softly. "I remember."

Seeing Tir continuing to struggle, Serena hurried to the armory, replaced the disk, retrieved the strength belt, and buckled it around Tir's waist. Stepping back, she faced Tir.

"When Argent speaks, repeat what he says. Move your mouth but don't use your voice," Serena said. "I'm casting a spell so that I can capture and vocalize the words."

Tir nodded and began to move his mouth.

"We need more weapons," Serena said, repeating Argent's words that Tir heard. "You have your food. You have your animals. You have your treasures. Now keep digging."

A pause. Serena momentarily glanced at Marlys as she waited for Tir to continue.

"No, you can't move the star monument. It's the only way to get back there. I don't care if it makes digging harder. Do it!"

As Serena spoke, Celestine rushed to the classroom and returned with paper, pen, and inkwell. She placed them on a nearby stand and began to write.

Serena continued to repeat Argent's words. "Get me a new jacket. Those miscreants tried to attack me, but I outwitted them."

Another pause.

"This time we'll get them all. Take what we need and burn the rest. All will bow down to me."

Marlys saw the pointer shaking violently in Tir's hands. Despite the strengthening belt, he seemed to have trouble holding it. Apparently, the device was not meant to easily handle the strain from bridging the gap between one world and another.

"Don't stop until you find it!" Serena said.

Tir gasped and dropped the pointer. It clattered to the floor. "Sorry, Marlys. I was afraid it was going to break in my hands and we'd lose it completely. We may need it again."

Marlys put a hand on Tir's shoulder. "You did more than anyone could have expected. Thank you."

Tir sank into a chair.

"You, too, Serena," Marlys said, as Serena also took a seat. "Thanks to both of you, we know even more about what he's up to now."

Celestine stood, holding her paper. "Digging? Did the sorcerers sent there bury their weapons?"

"Wouldn't they want to use them again?" Rochelle asked.

"It's been centuries upon centuries," Tir said. "Objects left on the ground get buried naturally over time."

"More likely they buried them so no one else could take them," Thorne said. "People commonly put valuables in a box, dig a hole, and then cover it to keep their possessions safe."

Marlys nodded. "Farmers and hunters commonly find old abandoned boxes in fields or ditches. My father said the owners probably died before retrieving them, or forgot about them."

"Whatever reason," Serena said. "The weapons were in the ground and Argent somehow uncovered them."

"Since he's been in the island worlds for so long, it probably took him all this time to find them and uncover them," Durand said.

"Not all of them," Rochelle said. "From the sound of it, he expects to find even more."

Celestine consulted her paper again. "Star monument? He said that's how he gets back here."

Marlys turned to Serena. "Have you ever heard of anything of this nature?"

Serena shook her head. "Let me check with Genevieve."

She opened a sorcerous channel. They could see Genevieve's image.

"Genevieve," Serena said, "we've discovered that Argent uses something he calls the 'star monument' to return here. Have you ever heard of such an artifact?"

"No." She raised her head and turned away. "Blair, Nessa, have you ever read of a star monument, or a way to return here from the island worlds?"

They heard Blair's voice. "No, and we've been searching intently."

Genevieve turned back to Serena, shaking her head. "Sorry."

Serena took a deep breath. "Genevieve, would you let me in the vault so that I can read the spell books there?"

Genevieve inclined her head. After a few moments, she said, "No one to my knowledge has read those books since the sorcerous wars. The spells recorded there are considered to dangerous for anyone to know, much less cast."

"I realize that," Serena said, "but we may have no choice but to consult them."

"Let me think this over. I need to discuss this with the other Librarians here," Genevieve said.

"Fair enough." Serena said. "May the Bright Beings guide you." When Genevieve nodded, Serena broke the connection.

"I think we would have to be desperate to consult those spell books," Celestine said.

"If I had the power to get there, I'd consult them," Thorne said.

Tir let out a chuckle as he covered his mouth. "Sorry." He turned to Thorne. "You have no idea what's in those books and how well they are guarded. Nessa and Zaria nearly were buried under a mountain of rocks just attempting to reach them."

"Then what would you propose?" Thorne asked.

Before anyone could answer, Celestine held up her notes again. "The last sentence we heard from Argent: 'Don't stop until you find it!' That sounds ominous."

Tir let out a breath. "I know. I wanted to hang on a few more moments to find out, but I couldn't."

"You did your best," Marlys said. "No one could have done better."

"He's looking for something," Durand said.

"But what?" Celestine said.

"I wonder if he also found a list of weapons and what they do," Serena said.

"Possibly," Marlys said.

"He also spoke of treasures," Celestine said.

"Probably referring to items they looted from Briarhill," Thorne said.

As they conversed, Marlys saw movement out of the corner of her eye. Stavros had padded softly down the stairs leading to the bedrooms, staying close to the walls. When he spotted Marlys staring at him, he ran to her, knelt at her feet, and bowed his head.

"Please have mercy, esteemed sorcerer. He said he would harm my wife and children."

Marlys reached down and drew him to his feet. "You aren't in any trouble. We know you were forced."

Stavros remained standing but kept his head down. "Let your wrath fall on me alone. My family is innocent."

Marlys reached over and put a hand on each of his shoulders. "We are not angry. You and your family are safe here. You're welcome to stay until we can find another safe place for you."

Stavros raised his head.

Marlys smiled at him and let go of his shoulders.

"Thank you." He stood. "I can work. I'm a good worker. I can tend animals. I don't mind cleaning stables. I can plant and weed and harvest."

Marlys inclined her head. "There is no lack of need in those tasks." She waved Astrid over. "Here. Your cart and horse are still outside. Astrid will show you where to put them. Our barns are within our protective barrier, so someone here will have to escort you in and out."

Stavros put a hand over his heart and bowed. "Thank you again. You are most kind."

Astrid gestured to Stavros to join her. They both left the room.

"The poor man was terrified," Lyra said when they had gone.

"After dealing with Argent, I'm not surprised," Thorne said.

Marlys looked at Thorne meaningfully. "There's still a feeling among some of the citizenry that sorcerers are to be feared."

Thorne lifted her chin. "I would say we were 'regarded.' But we didn't loot their shops or destroy their houses. I rid the continent of Argent long ago because of that. People were grateful."

"I'll give you that," Tir said.

Thorne turned to Durand. "You took Argent's knife. Would you allow me to see it?"

Durand removed it from his pocket and extended it to her, hilt first. "By all means."

Thorne placed the flat of the blade over a palm. "It's spelled, but crudely. Probably did it himself. Since he was never trained, he had to guess as to how to do it. It doesn't feel as if he put much effort into it."

"Can it do anything beyond what a regular knife would?" Rochelle asked.

Thorne looked up. "Oh, it can deliver a stronger thrust and resist breaking, but would do little more than a regular knife." She attempted to give the knife back to Durand, but he waved it away.

"Keep it. I have no use for such things."

Thorne shrugged and put it in a pants pocket.

"How did you and Durand put a knife in your pockets without hurting yourselves?" Lyra asked.

"I reinforce all of my clothes through magic," Durand said. "They last longer, don't tear, don't wear out."

"So do I," Thorne said. "Were you not taught the spell, child?"

"I taught it," Celestine said.

Lyra shrugged. "I just didn't see a need to use it on my clothes."

No alarms were raised the rest of the day. At suppertime, Stavros, Lena, and the children appeared. After setting the baby in a padded basket, and giving the toddler paper and charcoal to draw with, the parents helped with meal preparation. They ate at the table in the kitchen, helped with cleanup, and returned to their rooms. They did the same at breakfast the next morning.

Marlys approached them. "You're welcome to stay here as long as you wish, but there's no one for your youngsters to play with, and you may find the company of sorcerers tedious. Filix, in the town of Valleyview, has an inn. He's always looking for help with the food and the animals. There's a playground and school nearby for the little one, and some of the rooms at the inn have a nursery for the baby. Would you allow us to introduce you?"

Stavros and Lena faced each other. Lena nodded.

Looking up at Marlys, Stavros said, "Yes, that would be fine. Thank you."

Marlys gestured at Lyra. Nodding, Lyra led the family out to the barn to claim their horse and cart. She cast a distance-shortening spell to speed them to Valleyview town. She returned promptly.

At the fortress, everyone tended to their usual chores, though warily. Celestine conducted her class for the apprentices. Sorcerers went out in pairs to tend the animals, gather fruit from the trees, and harvest vegetables from their gardens. Others cleaned the fortress by sorcery. Nessa returned from the Library, saying she had found nothing further that might help them and preferred to join in the fight while Blair and the other Librarians continued their research.

Serena and Rochelle stood by the armory, discussing which weapons would best be used in an attack, and by whom.

As their discussion continued, Thorne turned to Marlys. "I dislike having to simply wait for Argent to show up and defend ourselves. I'd rather attack."

"How do we attack if we don't know where he is?" Marlys said.

"I've been casting the locator spell several times a day but haven't yet caught him here before he shows himself," Thorne said.

"The only way I know to attack him, take him by surprise, is to go to the island worlds ourselves," Marlys said. "We could do that, but how would we return? It could take us years to determine how that 'star monument' of his works."

"Hmph," Thorne said. "It probably did take him years. It wouldn't necessarily take us that long."

"I'm not ready to risk that," Marlys said.

Voni's image appeared in the room. "He's here! Argent's here! He's setting the forest on fire!"

"Stay behind the sorcerous barrier," Marlys said. "We'll be there as soon as we arm ourselves."

Serena and Rochelle reached for weapons. As planned, Thorne put on the chest protector, belt, and glove. She picked up the mace.

"Janna and Kelsie were already out in the woods when he appeared," Voni said. "Elspeth went out to bring them back. The rest of us are inside."

"Can you see him from where you are?" Marlys said.

"Yes, though the windows," Voni said.

"Does he have a battle axe?"

"Yes, he does. He's carrying a shield, too."

Marlys shuddered. "We'll be right there." Serena put the vambrace on Marlys's arm as she spoke. Rochelle handed her the bludgeon. Tir had the hammer. Serena grasped the trident and the stake. Rochelle grabbed the hook.

"I'll follow behind the put out the fire," Durand said.

"I will, too," Nessa said.

"I'll use the stake to put a barrier in front of us right away," Serena said to them. "Just stay behind it. The rest of us will have to move in front of it to attack, but we can retreat to its shelter if necessary."

"Why did he attack there and not here?" Lyra asked as they prepared to go. "He wants Thorne and he knows she's here."

Durand turned to her. "Because he failed here. He thinks he'll have success elsewhere and he knows Thorne will go anywhere to meet him."

Marlys cast the transportation spell. They emerged just outside the Valleyview training center. Immediately, Serena set a sorcerous wall around her and the Goldenvalley sorcerers.

A short distance away, Argent stood tall, holding the battle axe and shield. His men roamed in the woods, throwing lit torches into the brush. Argent set additional fires by magic. Marlys could already hear the wood crackling in the flames, smell the smoke going up, see ash falling.

With a loud cry, Thorne raced around the barrier and sprinted toward Argent, wielding the mace. Argent spotted Thorne, pointed the battle axe in her direction and made a chopping motion. Unaffected, Thorne pointed the mace at Argent and made a hammering motion. When this had no effect, she threw the mace at Argent. It bounced against the shield and fell to the ground. She thrust her gloved hand at Argent, but it did not gather the battle axe or the shield. Keeping an eye on Argent, she dived to retrieve the fallen mace.

A shout rang out from the woods. Janna ran toward Argent, casting a pushing spell, which caused Argent to sway from side to side. He recovered quickly and brandished the battle axe, facing Janna.

Elspeth came into view. She intercepted Janna and pushed her to the ground, out of Argent's line of sight. Turning toward Argent, she gathered herself to cast a spell. Argent swung the battle axe toward her and made a chopping motion. Elspeth collapsed.

"Elspeth!" Thorne exclaimed, charging toward her.

Before Argent could take any other action, Serena corralled him and the other men as if she had thrown a lasso around them. She quickly tightened the sorcerous rope. The men bounced against the perimeter helplessly as Tir aimed the terror hammer at them.

Seeing no way to advance, Argent opened the portal to the island worlds. All within Serena's boundary fell through it.

After the portal had closed, Marlys rushed to Elspeth. The elder sorcerer lay in the grass, eyes closed. Marlys knelt next to her as Janna crawled nearer, stopped, and sat up, staring at her mentor silently. Kelsie walked up behind Janna and sat beside her, putting an arm around Janna's shoulders.

Thorne dropped to her knees. She touched Elspeth's face and hair gingerly. She cast a healing spell, which had no effect. Lifting Elspeth's head and chest, she embraced Elspeth, sobbing. "Elspeth, oh, Elspeth, don't leave me! Don't go! You have to wake up."

Marlys sorcerously searched for a sign of life and found none. Elspeth's hand was within reach. Marlys clasped it, finding it still warm, but motionless. She cleaned Elspeth's body and preserved it though magic.

Thorne rocked back and forth with Elspeth still in her arms. Tears streamed down her face. "Oh, Elspeth, Elspeth! Whatever will I do without you?"

Marlys became aware of others gathering around her but did not look up. She heard gasps, sniffling, and soft exclamations of "oh, no." Eventually she faced the sorcerers surrounding her. "Are the fires out?"

Several heads nodded.

"Thank you." Marlys spotted Voni among those gathered.

"Is she...? Voni asked.

Marlys inclined her head.

Finally, after what seemed an eternity to Marlys, Nessa bent down and touched Thorne on the shoulder. "Aunt Thorne, we need to get Elspeth inside. She deserves a proper place to rest where others can come to mourn her."

Marlys rose to her feet to make room for Thorne to stand. She saw that all Valleyview sorcerers and apprentices had come outside. They appeared stunned.

Silently, painfully, Thorne gathered Elspeth's body in her arms, picked her up, and carried her to the training center. Voni opened the barrier to let her in and gestured to a long padded bench. Thorne gently placed Elspeth there and stepped back, maintaining vigilance over the body of her friend.

Serena, Rochelle, Tir, Zaria, and Durand stood respectfully at a distance, hands folded in front of them.

The Valleyview sorcerers and apprentices drew closer to the bench. Several comforted their colleagues with embraces. Many wept. Some stood rooted to the floor in shock.

Nessa walked to the kitchen and began to make tea, a process accomplished quickly through sorcery. Marlys walked over and helped her fill cups and put them on trays. They walked around offering the tea and giving what small gestures of comfort they could.

When Marlys reached the Goldenvalley sorcerers, Durand said softly, "In living memory and beyond, no sorcerer has been murdered, let alone by another sorcerer in battle."

"I think we all assumed this could never happen to any of us," Marlys replied.

Eventually, Marlys put the tray down. She took a cup of tea and walked over to Thorne, extending it.

Thorne turned on her savagely with a tear-stained face. "Why are you still here? You never liked her! You hated her!"

Marlys opened her mouth to say, "That's not true," but realized this was not the time and closed it again.

Nessa interposed herself between Marlys and Thorne. She put her arms around Thorne's shoulders and shook her head slightly.

Marlys nodded to show she understood that Thorne was not ready for a conversation with her. Lifting her head, she saw Durand motioning to her. He led her to Janna and Kelsie, who sat facing each other. Both had tear-stained faces and reddened eyes.

"It's my fault," Janna said. "It's all my fault."

"It's both our faults," Kelsie said.

Marlys bent down and put one hand on each of their shoulders. She turned from one to the other. "It's neither of your faults. The only fault is with Argent."

"But if we hadn't been out there...," Kelsie said.

"Neither of you could have known that Argent was about to appear," Marlys said. "You did what you thought you needed to do to protect yourself and others. Elspeth did the same."

Janna pointed to herself. "I was the one who drew his attention."

"So did the rest of us," Marlys said. "He could just as easily have killed any of us."

One of the other Valleyview sorcerers, Frieda, shouted across the room. "You Librarians! You're supposed to be so powerful!" She gestured toward Elspeth's body. "Why didn't you prevent this?"

"Do you think we didn't try?" Serena challenged.

"Not hard enough!" yelled an apprentice.

Durand held up a hand. "Recriminations will get us nowhere. We sorcerers, our apprentices, we are all siblings together. All of our hearts are broken when one of us dies, moreso if it happens in this terrible way. Let us grieve, yes, but let us grieve together, without divisions. The only one who benefits is the murderer, who would laugh if he saw us arguing like this."

"We have to do something," Voni said calmly.

"We will," Marlys said. "It may not seem so, but every sorcerer on this continent is determined to put an end to Argent."

"The sooner, the better," Thorne said bitterly.

Chapter 8

A group of Valleyview sorcerers placed a narrow bed in the middle of the main room. Thorne carried Elspeth's body there and laid it out gently. Many in the room gathered around. Marlys remained at a distance, looking at Elspeth's body. She appeared to be merely in a deep sleep, except for the lack of chest movement.

Marlys turned and faced the sorcerers from the fortress. "Everyone needs to know about this. I need to go into another room and open the sorcerous channels." She leaned toward Voni, who was nearby. "May I invite those who wish to pay their respects to come here?"

"Of course." Voni nodded.

Marlys walked to Valleyview's classroom, empty now, and took a seat behind one of the desks. The sorcerers from the fortress took seats around her. Placing a hand to her forehead, she took a moment to collect her thoughts.

Durand leaned toward her. "I can make the announcement if you open the sorcerous channels for me."

She lowered her hand. "Thank you, but no. I'm High Sorcerer for Goldenvalley. It has to be me." She took several deep breaths and used what magic she could to calm her nerves.

Steeling herself, she opened the sorcerous channels to every fortress and training center on the continent.

"This is Marlys, High Sorcerer of Goldenvalley. I require your attention." After giving her hearers a moment, she took a ragged breath and continued. "There's been a death among the sorcerers here. Argent came to Goldenvalley and murdered Sorcerer Elspeth." She paused, hearing gasps and exclamations of horror. "She died heroically, shielding another sorcerer from Argent's killer weapon, but was unable to avoid it herself."

She paused again, briefly placing both hands on her forehead to forestall tears. Could she keep herself together to make a simple announcement?

"We will have a traditional sorcerer's memorial. You are welcome to visit here to pay your respects any time within the next day. If you are beyond the reach of an end point spell, we can send Librarians to bring you here."

Genevieve spoke up. "I can speak for every Librarian in this District. Any of us are willing to transport any of you to Valleyview and back. Just ask."

"Thank you," Marlys said. "If you will excuse me, I need to return to attending to matters here. Open a channel to me if you wish to speak further." She closed the channel, buried her head in her hands, and wept with abandon.

Serena took a chair next to Marlys and put an arm around her.

When Marlys's tears were spent, she lifted her head, put a hand in her pocket, and drew out a handkerchief. She wiped her face and blew her nose.

Voni walked in. "Marlys? Serena?"

"Yes?" both said at once.

"I'm not assigning blame, I'm just curious," Voni said hovering over the table. "Don't you have the ability to block a spell?"

"I do," Serena said firmly, "and I've tried to use it. The problem is, Argent isn't casting spells except to return to the island worlds. He's using sorcerous weapons."

"I understand that you have to be a sorcerer to use those weapons?" Voni asked.

Serena nodded. "You do. But it's not the same as casting a spell. Would that it were so I could block it."

Voni nodded.

"I just told the entire sorcerous community that they could come here to pay their respects. I added that we would have a traditional memorial for Elspeth," Marlys said. "I presume that's your intention?"

"Yes," Voni said. "Elspeth would have wanted a traditional funeral."

"You'll have to have to assign door wardens to let the visiting sorcerers through the barrier," Serena said.

"Done," Voni said. "They've already started to arrive. And Marlys?"

"Yes?"

"All of us here know you didn't hate Elspeth. She spoke fondly of you, and I know that you respected her."

"Thank you," Marlys said. "Oh, by the way, I didn't see Celeb and Jessie. Are they around?"

"A family in Valleyview town took them in. Elderly couple. They were happy to have someone to help with cooking and cleaning in exchange for shelter. All of the other citizens who were here have been similarly housed. The townspeople have been generous in opening their doors. Only sorcerers and apprentices are here at the moment."

Marlys nodded.

Voni straightened and started toward the door. When she did so, Marlys saw Janna and Kelsie enter the room, Kelsie in the lead.

Kelsie stopped and nodded. "High Sorcerer Marlys. Sorcerer Voni."

Hearing the formal address, Marlys knew that a request was coming.

"Yes, Kelsie?" Voni asked curiously.

"I want to become a sorcerer. Now."

Voni glanced at Marlys, then back to Kelsie. "We can't do this now, Kelsie. We all need to finish mourning Elspeth first."

"But Elspeth always wanted me to become a sorcerer."

"She did," Voni said, "but we need to be respectful of everyone else."

"And we have to plan a celebration at the fortress," Marlys said.

Kelsie waved a hand. "I don't need one. I just want to be a sorcerer."

"To take revenge on Argent?" Serena asked.

Kelsie scratched her right temple. Her sheepish expression told Marlys that Kelsie felt embarrassed to admit it aloud.

"We all want to see Argent pay," Rochelle said. "But this sort of fight needs sorcerers with experience."

Kelsie gestured at Janna. "But Janna went to fight."

"Janna went with me and Thorne and several other experienced sorcerers," Marlys pointed out.

Kelsie lowered her eyes and bowed her head. "Thorne would let me become a sorcerer," she murmured.

Voni sighed. "We'll wait until after the memorial."

Kelsie raised her head.

Voni put a hand on Kelsie's back and Janna's back. "For now, let's join the others." She pushed them gently toward the door.

"That won't end well," Tir said. "She seems determined to do something rash."

"She has to break through our crucible first," Rochelle said. "Not everyone does the first time."

Marlys pushed her chair back and stood. "I'm not sure I could endure another funeral."

"I don't think any of us could," Durand said. He and the others Goldenvalley sorcerers ambled to the door.

When they were out of the room, Serena rose from her chair. She leaned toward Marlys and murmured in her ear. "Marlys, no matter what the Librarians in the District decide, you and I are going to the vault and opening it. I'm going to read the forbidden spell books."

Marlys realized that Serena had not asked permission. In the next moment, she understood that Serena knew that they were of the same mind. After exhaling slowly, Marlys said, "Yes. I agree."

They cemented their agreement with a meaningful nod and quick meeting of their eyes. Purposefully, they rose and left the classroom.

When Marlys reached the main room, she found it more crowded than when she left it. The room was abuzz with low conversation. Thorne had taken a seat near Elspeth's head. She did not take her eyes off the body.

Looking around, Marlys saw a number of sorcerers with auras: the sign of Librarians.

Serena leaned toward Marlys. "Sorcerers from the Library District, come to pay their respects, I presume."

Marlys nodded.

Brianna walked toward them with a tray of waycakes and cups of tea. "Eat a waycake. You'll feel better."

Marlys and her companions each took one.

"Thank you," Marlys said.

"It's the least we could do in light of such terrible news." Brianna turned. "All the station hosts are here. Librarians from the District offered to mind the Spell Passage so we could come."

"We're glad you came," Marlys said. "Thank you."

Brianna inclined her head and continued on her path with the tray.

Marlys joined the assembly crowded around Elspeth's bed. She stood there, staring, unmindful of the time, until she felt a touch on her shoulder.

"Marlys," Niquelle said, "all the high sorcerers on the continent are here. We should talk."

Marlys motioned with her head. "The classroom is over there."

Niquelle turned and gestured to the other high sorcerers to follow. They moved toward the classroom door, waving off their aides.

Just before Marlys entered the room, Genevieve stepped next to her and beckoned to Serena.

"We have need of Serena, too," she said.

They were the last ones in the room. Genevieve closed the door behind them. All the sorcerers began to move tables and chairs until they formed a square so that those in attendance could face each other. Marlys noticed that the station hosts, too, had joined them.

When all were seated, Genevieve said, "I know we are all heartbroken. But we must discuss our next moves, and we must do it now."

Marlys heard sounds of agreement.

Niquelle started the discussion. "I have walled off every town, training center, and farmstead in my region, No one is going in or out until this threat has passed."

"I have done the same," Ware said, "but we can't stay within sorcerous barriers forever. Trade is necessary. Harvesting is necessary."

"All that can be done by moving citizens through end points," Divira said. "Awkward and time-consuming, but it can be done."

"This is ridiculous," Lindra said. "One sorcerer disrupting an entire continent?"

"Any experienced sorcerer gifted with extraordinary strength can cause widespread damage," Genevieve said. "Marlys, Serena, or I, working alone, could devastate a region in a matter of days."

"That's the reason for the orbs along the spell passage," Yvette said.

"That's the reason we're all pledged not to harm each other," Ware said, "else one sorcerer could eliminate all the others."

Marlys scratched an eyebrow. "Equally, it's the reason that Thorne's high sorcerer made an exception and pledged her only not to harm a sorcerer similarly pledged."

Niquelle turned to Marlys. "Keeping at least one sorcerer who can harm a rogue is something we need to consider going forward."

"Right now, we have three: Thorne, Zaria, and Janna," Marlys said. "Though when this crisis is over, we may wish to reduce that number."

"Or we may not," Niquelle pointed out.

"Maybe, in addition to pledging ourselves not to harm other sorcerers," Lindra said, "we might think of pledging ourselves not to harm citizens, either."

"I bound Nessa to such an oath." When all eyes turned to her, Marlys added, "Before leaving that subject, by the way, could you release Nessa from being banned from the regions? I think she's more than earned her redemption." She saw nods and heard sounds of assent.

"However," Ware said, "we should not pledge sorcerers not to harm citizens regularly. Rogue sorcerers? Maybe we see one once in a century. Rogue citizens? Every few years or so, at least in my region."

Again, Marlys heard sounds of agreement.

"Back to the subject at hand," Ilse said, "what do we do about the rogue sorcerer we have now? As Lindra said, we're having enough difficulty with the one. Makes me wonder how the world survived with an army of such."

"The world almost didn't survive," Genevieve said. "That's the reason my long-distant predecessors walled off the Library District and made it next to impossible to get in. Barring District Librarians organizing a rebellion, which we take great pains to prevent, no such sorcerous army can reach us, much less a single rogue."

"Why the isolation, though?" Ware asked. "There was no communication or visitation for so long that many thought that the Library of Sorcery didn't exist."

"From what I've read of our own archives, two reasons," Genevieve said. "First, remaining at the Library for more than a few days will increase one's sorcerous powers significantly, as you can see with Marlys and Serena, here. My predecessors were wary of having large numbers of exceptionally strong sorcerers all across the continent, and I will add that many in the Library District still feel that way. Many feared that this could cause an ambitious sorcerer to raise another sorcerous army to conquer the world."

"And the second reason?" Edwina asked.

"There was some dispute at the time between the District Librarians and the areas outside the District. As the station hosts will tell you, the area including the Spell Passage has long been opposed to any sort of hierarchy, which my predecessors thought was risky. As for the regions, my predecessors felt that the High Sorcerers were not making sufficient efforts to keep the sorcerers in their area from dominating and exploiting the citizens."

"Yet we in the Spell Passage area have found that both sorcerers and citizens feel well served," Clea said.

"As for those of us in the regions," Lindra said, "we aren't perfect, but we do try."

Genevieve nodded. "Granted. I was answering your questions by reporting what I understood the attitude was at the time."

"Again, we still need to discuss what to do about Argent," Ilse said.

"We're willing to help if what you need is more sorcerers," Ware said. "But it seems as if Argent is focused on attacking Briarhill and Goldenvalley. Furthermore, Goldenvalley has the sorcerous weapons that have been keeping him from overwhelming us, and they know how to use them. I'm presuming there is no great cache of weapons that can be distributed to the rest of us?"

"Correct," Marlys said.

"In that case," Ware said, "it seems that the best course of action at the moment is to leave the weapons with Goldenvalley and have them take the lead. The rest of us can and should stay behind our barriers until we are needed."

"I take for granted that Goldenvalley will come to our aid if Argent comes to our regions," Niquelle said.

"Absolutely," Marlys said.

Ilse looked around the room. "I'm sensing that none of us has a plan to counter Argent, except to watch for him and oppose him however possible whenever he appears."

"We've had success at keeping the peace for years uncounted," Divira said. "The result is that none of us have any experience at battle strategy."

"Though we remain open for anyone to contribute any ideas," Marlys said.

"We are researching the sorcerous wars at the Library to see if we can learn something from how they were defeated," Genevieve said.

"Then we will leave that to you." Ilse said.

Marlys saw nods and gestures of agreement. "Having reached a consensus, let us continue to honor our fallen sister."

All stood and returned to the main room.

The rooms in the training center remained crowded, especially when apprentices from other places started appearing with sorcerers. Marlys was glad that the apprentices had a chance to pay their respects as well. They went home when the sorcerers in their areas did.

Eventually only local sorcerers and apprentices were left. Thorne remained seated by the body.

"She hasn't moved," Durand said softly to Marlys.

Marlys turned to Voni. "Why don't you ask if she wants to stay here tonight?"

Voni nodded and approached Thorne. When Voni gave her proposal, Thorne nodded.

Durand approached Thorne as Voni gave directions for the others to move a bed into the room. He bent toward Thorne. "Why don't you take a walk outside, take the air? The protective barrier includes the grounds around the building here."

Stiffly, Thorne got to her feet. Durand assisted her. Without looking at anyone, Thorne slowly walked to the back door. Marlys heard crickets and felt the cool night air come in when the door opened.

With Thorne gone, Marlys took the opportunity to move closer to Elspeth. She sat in Thorne's chair and put a hand on Elspeth's head, stroking her hair. "I'm so sorry, Elspeth. I'm so sorry." She stood as sorcerers and apprentices moved a bed nearer.

"Do you want to stay here overnight as well?" Voni said.

"No, I'll sleep in my own bed," Marlys said. "I'll come tomorrow morning for the funeral."

"We'll have everything ready," Voni said.

Marlys called for those residing in the fortress to gather. She opened an end point and they all returned home.

Once there, they all silently, wearily separated. Some went to the kitchen, others to their rooms. Marlys trudged to her suite, strangely empty without Thorne there, though they had separate rooms. She took a long, hot bath, lingering in the water until it began to grow cold. Once out, she toweled herself off and put on a nightgown. For a time, she sat at the edge of her bed, weeping. Eventually she dried her tears, stretched out on the bed, covered herself, and slept.

The next morning, without consulting each other, apprentices and sorcerers alike dressed in their finest robes. Marlys opened an end point, and they all walked through. The empty fortress would be well guarded by the protective spell.

When they arrived at the Valleyview center, they found preparations already underway. Thorne's bed had been removed.

When Voni saw Marlys, she approached. "It's time to take off the preservation spell."

Marlys nodded, stepped forward, and put a hand on Elspeth's body. Before she could release the spell, Thorne leaned over and put a hand on hers. Their eyes met.

"We have to let her go, Thorne," Marlys said.

"I will act as the lead mourner at the memorial," Thorne said.

"Of course," Marlys said.

Thorne lifted her hand and stepped back.

Once Marlys released the preservation spell, Voni and others at Valleyview came forward to wrap Elspeth's body in silken fabric, secured with matching cords. Carefully, they carried the body outside. Everyone followed.

A grave had been prepared within the barrier. The carriers lowered the body in the hollow using the cords. Thorne moved within a step of the edge, gazing downward.

Marlys turned from side to side. All the apprentices and sorcerers from Goldenvalley stood there, joined by the High

Sorcerers of all the regions. Durand and Clea represented the area along the spell passage. Genevieve and Blair stood for the Library District.

Thorne raised her arms. Her back was to the assembly. She remained facing the grave. "We honor you, Elspeth."

"We honor you, Elspeth," everyone repeated.

"You will remain in our memory." Again, repeated.

"We release you to the glorious realm of the Bright Beings."

Janna and Kelsie stepped forward carrying a pear tree sapling, readied for planting. The two held it in place as the sorcerers filled the grave with soft earth from the mound created when the grave was dug. Once the tree had been secured in the fresh ground, they stepped back.

Nessa moved forward. She vocalized the traditional farewell for a fallen sorcerer, a wordless melody whose origins had been lost in time. Other singers, including Durand, joined her in the chorus.

When they finished, Thorne turned. "Thank you, all, for honoring our sister. Please join us in a feast to celebrate her memory."

Everyone went inside, where a large table had been set. Thorne sat at the head of the table and received condolences from the visitors as the meal progressed. Marlys and those who knew Elspeth well and wished to speak shared their experiences, rising one after the other to address the gathering.

Marlys, as High Sorcerer of Goldenvalley, had the next-to-last opportunity to speak. "Elspeth acted to the best of her ability as she understood it to advance the sorcerous community and prosper all within Goldenvalley. I did not fully understand this at first, but I do now, and for that, I am grateful."

Thorne, as lead mourner, had the last word. "Elspeth was not only a great sorcerer, but a great friend. The world keenly feels her loss. May the Bright Beings welcome her into their arms."

Chapter 9

Thorne and Marlys bid the visitors farewell as they opened portals to their respective homes. When they were gone, Marlys moved to open an end point to the fortress, but Voni interrupted.

"A word with you before you go?" Voni asked, nodding to Marlys and Thorne.

Marlys turned to Serena. "Would you mind opening the way back to the fortress?"

"I'd be happy to." Serena cast the transportation spell. She and the other sorcerers from the fortress disappeared into it. Marlys and Thorne stayed behind.

Voni turned to one side.

Marlys could see Janna and Kelsie lingering behind her, wearing humble expressions, which Marlys felt were probably feigned.

"Kelsie wants to enter the crucible to become a sorcerer," Voni explained.

"You're the trainer here," Marlys said. "It's your decision to make."

Thorne scowled at Kelsie. "What are you trying to do? Get yourself killed?"

"No," Kelsie squeaked. "I want to fight."

"...which will get you killed," Thorne said. "Leave the fighting to your elders."

"I still want to be a sorcerer," Kelsie said. "You've all been saying it's past time that I tried."

Thorne faced Voni and let out a heavy sigh. "Oh, let her try. Most apprentices don't break through the first time anyway."

"Marlys?" Voni asked.

"Still your decision," Marlys said.

Voni shrugged. "All right. We have a crucible built and ready. You can try any time you want."

Kelsie grinned, clapped her hands, and bounced on her heels. "I'll try now." When she noticed the older sorcerers glaring at her, she added cautiously, "If it's all right with you?"

"Outside." Voni gestured.

Kelsie hurried out the front door, accompanied by all the apprentices. The group chatted gleefully as they rushed out. Marlys, Thorne, and Voni trailed behind, followed by Janna.

The crucible for testing sorcerers was a small, narrow shed. Whoever was inside would not have been able to stretch their arms to full length. Kelsie eagerly opened the door, stepped inside, and closed it behind her. Voni, Marlys, and Thorne came forward. Voni sealed the shed with sorcery as Marlys and Thorne stood by.

"Kelsie?" Marlys called when Voni finished.

"I'm here," came a muffled voice.

"Extend your powers and try to break through," Marlys said. "Take your time. If you're still at it an hour from now, we'll open the door and you can try again in a few days."

"I'll do it now," Kelsie said.

Marlys did not answer. She and the other sorcerers walked away so they would not be hit by flying debris if Kelsie managed to emerge. When they felt they had reached a safe distance, they turned to watch the shed.

The apprentices had gathered near them, chattering excitedly, speculating as to how long it would take Kelsie to break through.

Voni nodded to Thorne and Marlys. "You can go back to the fortress if you wish. We'll keep watch here and tell you if Kelsie succeeds."

"I think I can wait a little long—," Marlys began

Boom!

Debris flew everywhere. The sorcerers deflected the flying shards; the apprentices ducked to avoid them.

Janna ran forward and knelt by Kelsie, who was squirming on what used to be the shed's floor. "You did it!"

Kelsie, covered by wood dust and splinters, groaned loudly. "It hurts," she said hoarsely. "Everything hurts...so badly."

By that time, Marlys, Thorne, and Voni had reached Kelsie's side.

"You've seen sorcerers emerge from a crucible before," Thorne said. "The pain should not have surprised you."

"I didn't know it would be this bad," Kelsie croaked. Slowly, she rolled over on her back.

Thorne sighed and shook her head. She briefly met Voni's and Marlys's eyes before picking Kelsie up. Marlys saw that Thorne still wore the strength belt, though sorcerers could use magic to bear heavy burdens.

The apprentices cheered and surrounded Thorne as she carried Kelsie inside. Marlys, Voni, and Janna followed. Janna pulled aside the blanket on Kelsie's bed as Thorne set her there and sorcerously cleaned off the dust and splinters on Kelsie's hair and clothes. Once Thorne had tucked the blanket around Kelsie and used a healing spell to ease Kelsie's pain, she patted Kelsie's arm gently. "You'll feel better in a few days, child."

"Congratulations," Marlys said.

Kelsie smiled weakly and closed her eyes.

Marlys and Thorne bid farewell to the Valleyview assembly and returned to the fortress. As Thorne took off the strength belt and returned it to the armory, Celestine stepped forward.

"Nothing wrong at Valleyview, I hope," she said.

"No," Marlys said. "Kelsie wanted to become a sorcerer right away, so we indulged her."

Tir smiled. "Still in the crucible when you left?"

"She burst through almost immediately," Thorne said, joining the group.

"Um…doesn't that indicate great sorcerous power?" Rochelle asked.

"Yes," Thorne said. "If only she had the wisdom to match."

"She is on our side," Zaria pointed out.

"Wisdom can come in time," Durand said.

"Let's hope it comes sooner rather than later," Marlys said.

The remainder of the day was quiet. Thorne continued to cast the locator spell at intervals, but did not detect Argent's presence. In the morning, Astrid, who continued her nightly watch, reported no disruptions.

"According to what I learned through the sorcerous channels," she said, "there's no one on the roads. Sorcerers throughout the continent have surrounded the towns and major farmsteads with protective spells. Smaller farmsteads and distant cottages have been evacuated."

"It's the same in Goldenvalley," Celestine said. "I've done a thorough survey."

"Maybe if he finds he can't get anything, he'll give up?" Lyra ventured.

"He won't," Thorne said.

In the afternoon, Thorne approached Marlys as she sat at her desk. "He's here."

Marlys twisted around in her chair. "Where?"

"At the bend of the Crystal River."

Marlys slid her chair back and stood. "Let's see what he's up to."

As they walked toward the armory, Thorne said, "I take it we are in agreement that we need to observe him before attacking."

"Or instead of an attack," Marlys said. "If we can divert him or frustrate him, that could cause him to desist, at least for a while."

"Anything to prevent any further damage to the land and to prevent any more deaths among us," Thorne said.

"We've managed to get him to retreat back to the island worlds," Marlys said.

"If only we could get him to stay there," Thorne said.

"I doubt it," Marlys said. "His goal seems to be to rule the continent, beyond getting revenge on you."

When they reached the audience room, Thorne walked straight to the map. "I can place myself here," she said, pointing, "and cast a concealing spell. I doubt that he'll see through it." She snorted. "Come to think of it, I doubt that he knows a concealing spell exists."

Serena, Tir, and Rochelle quickly joined them. When Marlys threw them a questioning look, Serena said, "We all have you under a tracing spell. We knew what you were doing."

"We didn't want you to take off somewhere without us," Rochelle added.

"I take it Argent has appeared again?" Tir said.

Marlys nodded.

"I am going alone," Thorne said.

"No, you aren't," Marlys said mildly. "If he's at this bend of the Crystal River, and you're here, I can be here, and," she looked at Serena, "Serena can be here. That creates three points of a triangle on hills overlooking the river. We will all be able to observe and act from there."

"I can wear the chest protector," Thorne said, "that will keep him from killing me. But what about you two?"

"We can cast concealing spells, too," Marlys said, "and to keep us safe from him sweeping the area with the battle axe, we can take the stake. I'll go with Serena and put a barrier around me, hand Serena the stake, and then she can go to her location and put a barrier around her."

"You may have to step outside the barrier to cast a spell or use a weapon," Rochelle said.

"If I can keep the barrier between me and Argent," Marlys said, "I should be able to cast spells behind it or around it and remain protected."

"Besides," Serena said, "with the three of us in three different directions, he'll have his back to at least two of us at a time. That means he can use line-of-sight spells in only one direction."

Marlys stepped to the weapons display. "I'll take the vambrace and the bludgeon."

"I presume that Thorne is taking the mace, chest protector, and strength belt," Serena said. "I'll take the trident, the baton, and the glove."

"If he has that shield again, you won't be able to take the battle axe away with the glove," Thorne said.

"The glove has other uses," Serena said.

After fastening the vambrace on her forearm, Marlys scanned the armory display, seeking other options. "Wait. I have another idea." She picked up the lance.

"Tethering weapon?" Serena queried.

Marlys scrutinized the lance. "Yes." She faced the others. "Our aim, if Argent isn't being aggressive, is to gather information. Instead of spreading ourselves out on arrival, all three of us can emerge with Thorne on her hill. We can conceal ourselves and set the barrier in place. From there, I can point the lance at him and see if we can learn anything."

"What if he's already wreaking havoc?" Thorne asked.

"Then we return to our original plan," Marlys said.

Serena gestured to Thorne. "If Marlys has the lance, then give her the strength belt, just in case."

Thorne considered a moment before taking the belt off and handing it to Marlys. "If he goes back to the island worlds, you should be able to be tethered to him a little longer."

As they discussed their plans, Marlys noticed other sorcerers coming into the room and gathering around, listening.

"May I say that I prefer this plan?" Celestine said. "I wasn't fond of the idea of our two strongest sorcerers exposing themselves to possible combat and death without a tactical group with them."

"Presuming I'm expendable?" Thorne asked ironically.

"Not at all," Celestine said. "I'm only pointing out that our successes have been when we've employed several sorcerers at once."

"You still have Librarians here in our absence," Serena pointed out.

"True, but I'm with Celestine," Tir said. "I'd much prefer a larger group if you're going to fight him. I'm much more comfortable with a smaller group if the objective is to gather information."

"Whatever we do, let's do it now, before he disappears again," Thorne said.

"Agreed." Marlys opened an end point.

As planned, they stepped out on a wooded hill overlooking the bend of the Crystal River. To Marlys's relief, she saw no fires. Even though the trees adequately shielded them from view, they all quickly cast concealing spells and set a wide barrier around them before stepping out at a point where they could view the river bend clearly through the vegetation. Argent stood at the bank. His men milled around him.

"They seem to be just walking around on the far side of the river," Serena said.

"I see Argent has the battle axe, and the shield," Thorne said.

"He's talking to someone." Marlys raised the lance. "Let me point this at him and see what the conversation is about."

"Move your mouth so we can know what he's saying, too," Serena said.

Marlys nodded. She pointed the lance at Argent. Immediately, she heard his voice and repeated his words voicelessly.

"The sorcerers must have sealed the entire farmstead," Argent said, "if you and the men have been all around it without finding an entry point."

"No, I can't break it with a spell, or the battle axe here, I've already tried. I'd burn everything around it, except...yes, yes, I heard you, Grady. If I burn everything down, there won't be plants or animals to provide food when we take over. I understand that."

"You think you can find fruit trees and berries here in the wild? Just over there? Well, get to it then. Send those men over there. And some of the men can hunt? Maybe we can get food after all. See to it."

"Sorcerers? I wouldn't be afraid of them. After I killed one of them, they'd be fools to show their faces again. They won't bother us. Just get the supplies, fill the carts, and we can go back to our underground shelter. Yes, if we need wood, send someone to gather it. We have plenty of tools with us."

"No, we're not going back home, at least not now. We will go back later, though. We need more men to conquer. We need to establish a base here, first."

"I know you and the men want to go back where you came from, at least for a little while. I need to go back too, to see if I can find more weapons, more powerful weapons to aid in our campaign. No, you can't go back and forth by yourselves. I know that you can work the lever on the star monument, but nothing will happen unless you're a sorcerer and can open a portal. I have to be with you. Right now, I'm here. You're here. Now get to work."

Marlys saw the men separating into groups. The man called Grady seemed to be directing them. Argent kept on watch, looking from side to side, occasionally walking in a circle, surveying the surroundings.

Marlys held her breath when he briefly faced in their direction, but Argent gave no sign of spotting them and turned his attention elsewhere.

Marlys lowered the lance. "I have another idea," she said in a low voice. "Let's return to the fortress."

"Fine by me," Thorne said. "He doesn't seem to be destroying anything or killing anyone at the moment."

When they returned to the fortress, Serena and Thorne returned their weapons to the armory. Marlys removed the strength belt and extended it and the lance to Tir.

"Tir, take these."

He took the strength belt from Marlys and put it on. Grasping the lance, he said, "Who am I monitoring this time?"

"Me." Marlys turned to Serena as she grasped the chest protector and put it on. "Serena, you'll be in charge while I'm gone."

"Where are you going?" Serena asked.

"To the island worlds," Marlys said.

Chapter 10

Marlys heard several variations of "What?" or "Did you say you're going to the island worlds?"

"We can't be rash about this. It's too important," Thorne insisted. "We need to have a thorough discussion first. It's risky. It's unprecedented. No sorcerer has ever done this."

"We don't have time for that," Marlys said. "Argent is here, now. We must take advantage of the fact that he won't be there to find out what weapons he has access to. We have no way of knowing when he'll go back."

"We have no way of knowing if you can return here," Rochelle said.

"Argent made reference to a lever in the star monument," Marlys said. "That should be easy enough for me to find."

"What if you can't?" Celestine said.

"Then I linger, concealed if necessary, and wait for him to come back. He will return to this world eventually and I can go with him."

"How do you know that you'll emerge at his base?" Thorne said. "Whenever I have opened the portal to the island worlds, it seems to be different place every time."

"But is it?" Marlys said. "He seems to end up in the same place, or at least nearby. If I don't end up at that place, again, I can linger, keep casting a locator spell until he re-emerges, and go there."

"You've convinced me of the necessity of going there and the plan to return is sound," Serena said, "but I should go. It's still dangerous, and we can't spare you."

"Marlys is the one who needs to go," Durand said. "She has more sorcerous experience. If Thorne were a Librarian, I'd say she should go. Since Serena and Marlys are the ones here with the greatest sorcerous power, the scale tips to Marlys, as I see it."

"I agree," Tir said. "It's either Marlys or Serena, and Marlys has the depth of sorcerous knowledge. Besides, we'll be connected as long as my strength holds out, and can give advice if required."

"Marlys is a survivor," Celestine said, "she's faced desperate situations more often than any of us. She's best suited to handle this."

Marlys refrained from saying that she did not need anyone's permission to leave or that this was her decision to make. She simply noted others nodding and murmuring agreement. "I promise to be careful."

Serena leaned forward and embraced Marlys. "Be safe. I insist that you return."

When Serena released her, Marlys said, "I plan to, no matter what." She turned and walked toward the door.

"May the Bright Beings go with you," Serena called after her.

Others echoed the sentiment.

Marlys paused before exiting and briefly faced them. "Thank you."

Once beyond the protective barrier, Marlys opened a portal to the island worlds. Looking through the portal, she saw sunshine, a blue sky with white fluffy clouds, and green vegetation. Instead of rooting herself to the ground, as she always had done before when a portal opened near her, this time she allowed herself to be sucked inside and through.

After Marlys emerged on the other side, feet firmly on the ground, the portal closed behind her. The wind here was calm. Quickly, Marlys turned around. No one was in sight. She stood on a wide square paved with flagstones. On one side of the square, closest to her, she saw a manor house. On the other side stood a tall stone obelisk. A little farther away, she saw fields with tall corn and wheat, orchards, and a pasture with grazing cattle.

"The portal here has closed," Tir's voice said. "Are you all right?"

"Yes, I'm fine. I'm alone. Let me get my bearings and I'll report back soon." She walked toward the manor house. This stood two stories high and was fashioned of stone. Five large windows faced the front on the upper level. The middle window reached to the base and opened to a balcony over the door. At the lower level, Marlys saw windows on either side of the door, which was reached by stairs which led to a porch. The building appeared to be clean and well-kept.

Marlys ascended the stairs to the door. Before opening it, she listened for any sign of occupancy, but heard nothing. Enhancing hearing by magic, she still could hear no sounds of voices or movement near her, only the sounds of cattle in the fields. Reaching for the door handle, she found herself blocked by a simple spell, easily bypassed by a sorcerer, but impossible for a citizen to get around.

Slowly, carefully, Marlys pushed the door open and stepped inside. She found herself facing a staircase. A hallway beside the staircase reached to the back of the house. On either side open doorways revealed tidy rooms which were sparsely but elegantly furnished. She walked up the stairs, treading softly, and peeked into rooms on the second level, equally clean and well kept.

Entering the middle room with the large window, she looked out. At the far horizon, she spotted a city. Using a far-seeing spell, she confirmed multi-story stone, brick, and wooden buildings. Travelers walked or rode or drove carts to and from the city gates. A road stretched from there to a nearby village, just beyond the surrounding fields.

Fields and trees lined the road for a long way until the road reached a village close by. Again, Marlys could see people going about their business. A cluster of homes outside the village and closer to the manor house seemed to be farm houses, where women tended gardens, churned butter, and tended to animals. Children played in the open areas. Since she was inside, Marlys knew they would not notice her standing there, but doubted if they would notice her even if she stepped out on the balcony.

"It seems as if I'm in no danger of being disturbed," Marlys said to Tir as she descended the stairs and walked again on the flagstones in front of the house.

"What are you seeing?" Tir said.

Marlys strode close to the base of the obelisk and looked up. "There's a tall obelisk with a star shape embedded in it about halfway to the top," Marlys said. "I presume that's the 'star monument' Argent referred to. There's a large pit next to it, ringed by mounds of dirt. I'm going to see what's in it."

When she reached the edge, Marlys looked down. "I see glints of metal at the bottom. My guess is that these are from weapons yet to be unearthed."

"I'm repeating your words to the others," Tir said. "Serena wants me to tell you not to try to dig anything out. You might activate something accidentally."

"I agree," Marlys said. "I'm going back to the obelisk." She walked to the base and examined it closely. "It's tall, taller than our fortress, at least four stories."

"Do you see the lever Argent talked about?" Tir asked.

"Yes, it's on the side, within reach." Marlys brought her hand closer but did not touch it. "Protected by a simple spell. Only a sorcerer could grasp it."

"Any signs of writing?" Tir asked.

Marlys looked up. "There are indentations on the obelisk. One of the sides looks as if there's a ladder carved there."

"Can you climb up?" Tir asked.

"Not without a climbing spell. The lowest rung is far above my head. Besides, it's more an image of a ladder carved in the side than an actual ladder with hand and toe holds." She walked around the base, examining the four walls. "No writing here, either. There's a drawer on the base, within reach, sorcerously protected. I'm going to see if I can pull it out."

She broke through the spell and tugged at the drawer. It slid out, revealing an open book. "Ah! I think I've found the weapons list."

"Marlys, I've reached the end of my strength," Tir said. "I have to let go of the lance."

"Yes, I understand. I'm confident I can return."

"May the Bright Beings guide your way back."

Marlys's first thought was to remove the book and rush back to the fortress. Closing the book, she tried to lift it out of the drawer. It would not move. Using both hands, and enhancing her strength through magic, she tugged, putting all her might into the effort and leaning back. The book did not budge. Examining it for locking spells, she did not find one, or at least, one she could identify. She sensed no spell she could counteract. A spell to remove an anchored object did not work, either.

She could still open the book, close the book, page through the book, but the spine remained bound to the drawer. All attempts to move the drawer failed. Perhaps the book could be moved, but the time it would take to determine how to do it was not time she had to spare.

The only alternative she had was to remain as long as possible and read. She looked around to see if she could find anything she could use as a chair. There were chairs in the manor house, of course, but felt hesitant to remove them. Checking under the drawer, she saw another panel with a handhold. Pulling it out, she found it would work well as a seat.

Carefully, she paged through the book. A momentary thought crossed her mind that Serena might have been a better choice to send. The book was thick, and she doubted she could read through it in a reasonable amount of time. However, she had not gone far when she saw that the list of weapons ended, and what seemed to be notes began. She turned back to the list, which only took up a few pages.

The battle axe, shield, and charms were well documented. Other weapons mentioned included ones she knew about already. Either Argent had not used them yet, or had not found them yet. Omissions included the stakes creating protective barriers that Genevieve had brought form the Library. Perhaps only the Library had those, which was a relief.

Paging backwards instead of forward, she came across a page where "DESTROYED" had been written over the text in large red letters. Still, examining the text closely, she could read through the red ink to the black ink text and found that this section referred to the world-destroying weapon. Apparently, the losers in the sorcerous wars did not wish to ravage their new home, even accidentally. Marlys felt relieved.

She looked up at the obelisk. If the sorcerers of old could have come back to her world, their world of origin, why had they not used that power? Perhaps the book explained it elsewhere? Paging again, skimming the text, she saw that the lettering changed toward the end of the book. Skipping to the very end, she found blank pages.

Returning to the place where the text differed, she read, "Now I know why sorcerers record spells in a book. I try something, and I don't know what it was I did that worked, when it worked. Maybe if I write it down I can figure it out."

The miseries of a self-taught sorcerer, Marlys thought. *Learning by trial and error.* That had to be Argent's handwriting. The previous writing had been well-preserved, as were the pages and the binding. The letters were neater, too.

Reading the text as well as making inferences from the notes, Marlys discovered that the grounds surrounding the obelisk had been deserted when Argent arrived. Apparently the local townspeople, villages, and farmers avoided it. Argent quickly claimed residence of the manor house and used sorcery to get what he wanted, sometimes in trade for sorcerous help, sometimes with force. When he felt that he had the immediate area under his control, he attempted to widen his reach, only to be stopped by a company of other sorcerers. These came largely from the city on the horizon. They told him that he could practice sorcery unrestricted as long as he stayed where he was. If he were to venture elsewhere, he had to abide by their rules.

Argent grudgingly complied. He took the opportunity to ask questions. Their replies told him that the other sorcerers considered the manor house and obelisk worthless, obsolete. Relics of an era when a large group of other sorcerers came to this world. These sorcerers had found that wealth and power lay elsewhere, and prosperity rose when people were allowed to go about their business. Whenever new sorcerers came, they were instructed to follow the example of the established sorcerous community or be banished and confined to distant, harsh lands. The newcomers subsequently moved elsewhere and settled down to a more productive life.

His ambitions on the island worlds thwarted, Argent had only one other choice if he was to fulfill his plans and take revenge on the sorcerer who sent him there—he would have to return to the world of his birth. But how?

Day after day, year after year, he tried spell after spell to open a return portal. One day, in a tantrum of furious rage, he threw everything he had at the obelisk. It transformed. Instead of a tall spike sticking out of the ground, designs appeared on the side. The drawer and seat that Marlys had discovered were revealed. He discovered the spell book. He read the list of weapons.

Learning that the weapons had been buried, he concentrated on perfecting a penetrating spell. Marlys knew from her own experience that penetrating spells took years of practice before they worked well. In Goldenvalley, only she, Serena, and Celestine could claim proficiency. Argent, however, had years to develop his skill and was able to find where the weapons were buried. He was frustrated, though, by the fact that no sorcerer had yet invented a digging spell. For this, he needed laborers, and again persuaded or forced nearby villagers to start excavations.

At the same time, he tried various means to successfully open a portal back to the world of his birth. He learned through the spell book that by activating the star on the obelisk, he could observe the heavens. Perhaps if he could see other worlds in the void, he could see worlds separated by sorcery? There was a lever on the side of the obelisk, which he discovered could focus his sorcerous power if he pulled it and remained close to it while working spells. Like Nessa, he had already worked out an end point spell. Like Thorne, he had made up his own trap spell. Why not combine them?

So, it seemed, Argent had stumbled upon the correct combination. Activating the star, pulling the lever, then opening an end point spell within a trap spell could create a portal to send him back to the world where he originated.

Marlys smiled. A lucky accident, fueled by desperate determination. But he had done it. And so could she.

Chapter 11

Having learned the technique that would take her home, Marlys thought of using it immediately to go back. But since Argent and his men had not returned, and since she was still alone in the area, she felt she had time to gather even more information. Turning her attention to the spell book again, she paged to a section she had noticed had been crossed out in her previous browsing.

In contrast to the page which had "DESTROYED" written in red letters over it, the lettering in this section had black lines drawn through it. In the margins, the writing, which resembled Argent's script elsewhere, read, "Wrong! I tried with all my might, and nothing happened. This is false!"

Serena, their expert on books, had taught Marlys a spell which would allow her to read text that had been crossed out. She cast the spell. The words became clear.

"This device has magic both simple and complicated. The spell book may be accessed and read by any sorcerer. The upper levels have features which can only be read and used by the strongest sorcerers. Worthy ones may cast a spell to touch the sky."

Marlys had cast the "touch the sky" spell many a time. Nearly all sorcerers experimented with it. New sorcerers would have competitions to see how far up they could push an object. Inexperienced sorcerers generally could reach above the treeline. Stronger sorcerers, such as Celestine and Thorne, could reach the clouds. Marlys could reach into the upper atmosphere, near the interface with the void where the moon and stars orbited. According to Genevieve, there were sorcerers in the war even more powerful than she and Marlys and Serena.

Curious, Marlys decided to try it. She doubted that she could raise the obelisk from its base, but perhaps the point simply was to infuse the structure with magic. She closed the drawer holding the spell book, and replaced the seat inside the obelisk's panel. Stepping back to view of the pointed top, she cast the spell.

Almost immediately, the bottom rung of the ladder carving lit up. As Marlys poured more power into the spell, the rung above that brightened, then the one above that, until all the rungs shone. Carvings and indentations over the rungs began to glow. Soon, the entire obelisk, base to point, exuded a sorcerous aura.

Marlys knew from the quality of the illumination that this magical radiance could be only seen by a sorcerer. The top of the obelisk had to be visible to those in the nearby village, and a light might attract attention, or, worse, be reported to Argent upon his return. She did not wish Argent to know that she had been here.

"Welcome, sorcerer."

Startled by the voice, Marlys looked up. The sound reminded her of the time the weapons at the Overlook fortress had spoken to her. Loud enough for her to hear, but soft enough not to carry very far, Marlys remained still, hoping to hear more.

"There are many treasures within to uncover," the voice continued. "Use them wisely."

Marlys continued to look up, but heard nothing more. The sorcerous aura faded.

While she wondered how to access the treasures the voice referred to, she saw a glowing circle forming to her left. Quickly, she concealed herself.

Just in time. Once the loop was complete, men started pouring through it. Their clothes were drenched. Following a hunch, she ran toward the opening, avoiding the men, and stepped into the circle, passing Argent, just as he stepped out.

Marlys found herself standing in a field in the middle of a downpour. The circle had closed. There was no sign of Argent and his men except for footprints in the mud. Doing her best to ignore her skin, hair, and clothes getting soaked, she cast a locator spell to find Serena. Her destination confirmed, she cast a transportation spell to reach the fortress.

She appeared in the audience room near the armory wall. Quickly, she dried herself by magic, though she was not fast enough to avoid a puddle of water on the floor at her feet.

Everyone in the room turned to her. "Marlys!"

Marlys reached for the nearest chair and sank into it.

The others gathered around.

"What happened?" Lyra said. "Did you go for a swim?"

"No, it was raining at my return point." She looked out the window. "I see it's only cloudy here."

"I see you found the way to get back," Tir said.

"I found the method, yes," Marlys said. "The 'star monument' Argent mentioned was an obelisk with a star shape embedded on it. A sorcerer can use the star to scan the heavens. Cast a spell to activate the star, pull the lever on the obelisk, combine the trap and end point spells, and you can open a portal to this world."

"What do you mean by you 'found the method?'" Celestine asked.

"There's a spell book there. Argent recorded how he does it. I returned just now by going through the portal that Argent opened here to get back there. I concealed myself so they didn't notice."

"Then you didn't test the procedure," Thorne said.

"No," Marlys admitted.

"You said there was a spell book," Serena said. "You didn't bring it?"

"I couldn't remove it," Marlys said. "Brute force couldn't budge it. No spell that I tried worked."

"You got back safely," Tir said. "That's what counts. No sorcerer but Argent has ever done it before."

Marlys smelled freshly baked bread and realized she was hungry. She turned to the door of the dining hall. "I think the midday meal is almost ready. Let's eat. I'll tell you what I learned."

They all moved to the dining hall. When they were seated, apprentices came by with plates of vegetables and fruits, platters of baked chicken, and baskets of bread. Pitchers of cider and pots of tea had already been placed on the table. As everyone passed the food around and served themselves, Marlys gave a more lengthy account of her experience.

"Does that mean that the manor house and the obelisk have stood there all this time?" Lyra asked.

"Preserved by magic, I presume," Marlys said.

"I think it's significant that the sorcerers there didn't approve of Argent, either," Thorne said.

"But they left him there, nonetheless," Rochelle said.

"As long as Argent remained in the area around the obelisk," Thorne said.

"I feel sorry for the citizens living near him," Tir said.

"So do I," Marlys said. "But we aren't in a position to order their world."

"Defeating Argent would benefit both them and us, in that case," Serena said.

"An outcome greatly to be desired," Thorne said, "and as speedily as possible."

"I'm relieved that we don't have to worry about world-destroying weapons," Rochelle said. "The remaining weapons are nothing we don't know about already. But I wish we knew more about the treasures the obelisk spoke of. Those may work to our benefit. Especially since Argent doesn't have the strength to access them."

"To find out," Celestine said, "someone would have to go back to the island worlds, and I'm not in favor of that idea. Despite Marlys returning safely this time, it's still a risky move."

"I agree," Thorne said.

"I'm curious about what the obelisk has to offer myself," Serena said. "We may yet have to retrieve them. Still, we haven't exhausted all of the options available to us." She cast a meaningful look at Marlys.

"Which options are those?" Celestine asked.

Rochelle raised her head, took a deep breath, and faced Serena. "You want to read the forbidden spell books."

"It's about time someone did," Thorne said.

"Will Genevieve allow it?" Tir asked.

"Nessa and Zaria may not have been able to reach the spell books in the vault, but Marlys and I could," Serena said, "whether or not they gave consent."

"I'm not sure of the wisdom of trying that without their knowledge or permission," Durand said.

"How the Library District would react to our desire to read the forbidden spell books is something that is yet to be determined," Marlys said. "Genevieve, at least, said she would consider it. I'm not convinced that this is necessary yet. Niquelle thinks we can wait Argent out until he's exhausted his options. For now, this is something we can do. This course of action has the additional benefit of not creating any more casualties."

"I'm all for that," Durand said.

"We all are," Thorne said. "But if Argent doesn't relent, we will be forced to act again."

That evening, Marlys related her experience with those outside the fortress through the sorcerous channels. Everyone expressed astonishment that Marlys had gone and safely returned. Most showed interest in the obelisk.

"Of course, we knew that such structures could be built and imbued with magic," Genevieve said. "But there aren't any on this world, at least not that any records show."

"I wonder what 'treasures' the obelisk was referring to," Blair said.

"I had no chance to find out," Marlys said. "I saw no clue in the spell book, though I did not have a chance to read all the pages."

"Are you thinking of going back to find out?" Genevieve asked.

"Not at the moment," Marlys said. "We may have to eventually, but it's still a risky move, and we have no plans to do so."

"I wonder about the sorcerers who confronted Argent," Ware said. "It's rare for sorcerers to have progeny. Could they be descendants of those who participated in the sorcerous wars here, or are they sorcerers born of the original population of the island worlds?"

"It's possible they're descendants of sorcerers here who settled there," Marlys said, "though my guess is that they're born of the original population."

"Interesting questions," Ware said. "I'm curious as well, but I think our curiosity needs to be temporarily suspended until Argent is defeated."

"On the other hand," Lindra said, "the pursuit of seemingly trivial matters may lead to significant results."

"I'm all for gathering all the knowledge we can," Divira said. "But I agree with Marlys that there's no urgency to try to return to the island worlds now."

"Yes," Niquelle said, "I think it best to continue with our previously discussed plan of action."

Marlys nodded. "That is how we will proceed, then. We monitor, and we wait."

Chapter 12

The next day, while Marlys sat at her desk recording the previous evening's conversation, Voni contacted Marlys through the sorcerous channels.

"Kelsie has recovered," she said.

"Good," Marlys said. "Is she behaving herself?"

"She is not recklessly trying out her newfound sorcerous powers, if that's what you meant."

"That's what I meant," Marlys said.

"I've contacted you because everyone here wants a recognition ceremony for Kelsie," Voni said. "Even Kelsie, who said she didn't need one, is showing signs of changing her mind. If you think it's too soon after losing Elspeth, we'll just have one here at Valleyview. All of us think Elspeth would have wanted a ceremony for Kelsie."

Marlys suppressed a sigh. She took a moment to ponder the request. If the Valleyview assembly was in favor of a celebration, perhaps it was an appropriate time to hold one. "We'll have one here. I'll invite all of Goldenvalley to come. It will be their choice to attend or not. I have the feeling that all of the apprentices will be disappointed if there's no ceremony for Kelsie. They might begin to think there won't be one for them when they become sorcerers otherwise."

Voni smiled. "Thank you. When can you host a celebration?"

Marlys glanced out the window. Rain had started in Goldenvalley the day before, shortly after she returned form the island worlds, and showed no signs of letting up soon. "Tomorrow, I think. The weather will keep us indoors today in any case. Preparations will give us something to do other than to worry about when Argent will appear next."

"I'll tell everyone here," Voni said. "Thank you again." She closed the channel.

Thorne appeared at the open door. "I was listening. I don't think we could avoid a recognition ceremony for Kelsie, either.

Voni's right; Elspeth would have wanted one for her. Let's just hope that being surrounded by established sorcerers will inspire her to discipline herself."

"I hope so, too," Marlys said, though she still harbored doubts.

Once again, Marlys found herself with the prospect of presiding over a ceremony for a sorcerer she did not like very much. She kept telling herself that it was unworthy of her to feel resentment after all of these years. As High Sorcerer, it was her responsibility to look after the welfare of all the sorcerers and apprentices in her region, regardless of her personal feelings. Part of that included giving each of them their due recognition. Nonetheless, the task today was not one she could muster great enthusiasm for. But she took pride in carrying out her duties to the best of her ability, and was determined to do so this day as well.

The rain had stopped and the sun was out. Marlys stood at the top of the stairs at the main entrance. She opened the protective barrier as needed and greeted all who came in. Every sorcerer and apprentice in Goldenvalley showed up. Kelsie, looking radiant in an elegant ivory satin gown with gold piping, approached with Janna and Voni flanking her.

"Congratulations, again, Kelsie," Marlys said. "Voni and Janna will escort you to the audience room and I'll join you there when everyone has arrived."

"Thank you, High Sorcerer Marlys," Kelsie said with a wide grin.

Thorne, who had been waiting just inside the entrance, reached out and touched Kelsie's shoulder. "I'll join you, too, if you don't mind."

"I'm happy to have you stand with me," Kelsie said with genuine enthusiasm.

When the group had walked down the hall, Tir learned toward Marlys and spoke in her ear. "We're going to keep an eye on that one." He gestured to Serena and Rochelle, who stood nearby.

"So will I," Marlys said.

When all the guests had come inside, Marlys walked to the audience room, past the assembly, and up the stairs to the dais.

Voni and Thorne stood on either side of Kelsie and a pace away. Janna stood behind them.

Marlys placed herself in the gap between Thorne and Kelsie and put an arm around Kelsie's shoulder. She faced the assembly. "Please join me in welcoming Sorcerer Kelsie."

The guests cheered enthusiastically. The sorcerers from the fortress conjured the usual sparkling lights and falling snowflakes. Kelsie hurried down the stairs and walked into the crowd, who patted her on the back and shoulders, offering their felicitations.

Voni turned to Marlys. "I noted you didn't have her take the pledge not to harm another sorcerer."

Marlys met Thorne's eye briefly before answering. "We felt it was best to have another sorcerer who could battle Argent without restriction."

"We'd have to restrain her from doing so," Thorne grumbled.

Voni turned to look from an exuberant Kelsie back to Marlys and Thorne. "But can she avoid being attacked by Argent?"

"None of us can be sure that Argent won't attack us," Marlys said. "Kelsie, at least, would be able to fight back."

Thorne and Voni descended the stairs toward Kelsie. Marlys meandered toward the table the apprentices had moved in the audience room from the dining hall. This held plates of sweets and breads as well as cups of tea and cider. Marlys picked up a cup of cider and sipped while watching the rest of the room. Kelsie was the center of attention wherever she was. At other places, small groups of sorcerers gathered in conversation. Marlys felt relieved that Elspeth's death had not prevented them from honoring a colleague's accomplishment, though she knew that Elspeth was not far from anyone's mind.

Meanwhile, Kelsie drifted over to the armory wall, where Rochelle explained the weapons to a rapt audience. Marlys made her way over to stand at a spot where she could observe Kelsie.

"This is the deadliest weapon we have here," Rochelle said, taking the mace from the wall and holding it carefully. "It will cause unconsciousness like the knockout spell, but if the person isn't healed within a few days, the person will die."

"How do you activate it?" Kelsie asked.

"Point it at someone and make a hammering motion as if you were striking them," Rochelle said.

"Do you actually have to hit them?" Kelsie asked.

"No, the person can be at a distance." Rochelle placed the mace back on the wall and took out the chest protector. "This will prevent any spell or spelled weapon from affecting you. It molds itself to the one wearing it."

Thorne, who stood nearby with her arms crossed in front of her, added, "Argent has a magical shield which does the same thing."

Rochelle nodded and took out the vambrace. "If you wear this, you can cast a spell on someone wearing the charm to deflect magic."

"The charm Janna has?" Kelsie asked.

"Yes," Rochelle said. "But we're mostly attacking using sorcerous weapons now, and the charm won't protect against those."

"Some of the weapons have similar properties." Serena reached for the strength belt. "This will increase one's strength."

"Can't we already do that with sorcery?" Kelsie asked.

"We can," Serena said, "but this increases strength beyond that and doesn't require one to cast a spell." She took down the rod with the disk at the end. "This will increase the stamina of whoever it is pointed at."

Rochelle put her hand on the baton but did not move it. "This does the opposite. It makes one weaker." She pointed to the bludgeon. "This has a similar effect. It weakens limbs."

Tir reached over and took the hammer from the display. "This causes people to flee in terror. It works like the mace: just point and make a striking motion."

Serena put her hand on the trident. "This creates a sorcerous perimeter. I've been using it like a lasso."

Tir grabbed the glove and put it on. "This is nice." He held out his hand toward the javelin. It jumped off the wall and soared into Tir's hand, shaft first.

Marlys heard oohs and aahs from the onlookers.

"By the way," Tir added as he put the objects back on the wall, "the javelin will identify who's a sorcerer and who's not."

Kelsie pointed to the wall. "What does the giant hook do?"

Rochelle turned from Kelsie to the armory. "Oh, that. It moves objects from one point to another. Celestine and I have experimented with it. Yes, it can move a rock, or even a person, from here to there, but it doesn't seem to do more than what we can do with pushing spells."

"Those are more effective," Celestine added.

Kelsie's brow furrowed. "Oh, it has to do more than that. Why go to the effort to create a weapon that essentially does nothing? I think this has a lot of potential." She led out a hand. "May I try it?"

Rochelle turned from Kelsie to Marlys.

"Give it to her." Marlys threw Kelsie a stern look. "But test it outside."

Kelsie squealed with glee and grinned as Rochelle handed her the hook. She sprinted toward the door.

"Kelsie," Marlys called after her. "Someone here has to let you though the barrier surrounding the fortress."

Kelsie stopped, continuing to smile, as Marlys caught up with her and passed her. Marlys opened the door and created a gap in the barrier for Kelsie to pass through. She was followed by excited apprentices and perhaps a dozen sorcerers. After stepping through herself, Marlys joined the gathering and closed the gap behind her.

Outside, a gentle breeze blew through the grasses and ruffled the leaves on the trees. The sky was a brilliant blue and the sun shone down warmly. Near the barn, also protected by a barrier, the hens scratched in the yard while horses and cows cropped the grass in the nearby meadow. The area where Marlys and the others stood was a clearing between the fortress and the orchard.

Kelsie took a few steps away from the group. She held up the hook and looked around. Seeing a rock on the ground about ten paces away, she made a motion with the hook as if snagging it. "I'll see if I can move that rock." Slowly, she moved the hook to her left. The rock disappeared. Marlys and others looked around to see where it had gone. Kelsie, however, patiently continued to move the hook without interruption. The rock reappeared where the hook was pointing when Kelsie stopped moving.

Kelsie turned to Rochelle. "You didn't say the object disappeared in transit."

Rochelle shrugged. "It went from one place to another. What more is there?"

"Oh, there's lots more." Kelsie took a breath. "Does it work on a person?"

"We tried it, yes," Celestine said. "It's harmless. I barely felt anything when Rochelle turned it on me."

"Did you feel anything in between?" Kelsie asked.

"Nothing too different from how it feels to go through an end point," Celestine said.

Kelsie waved at a group of apprentices standing nearby. "Here. You go over there."

Five of them eagerly assembled at the place Kelsie designated.

"Now watch this!" Kelsie made a snagging gesture with the hook and turned a quarter circle. The apprentices disappeared and then reappeared when Kelsie stopped. Once they realized they had moved, the apprentices made noises of delight.

"That was incredible!" one said.

"Let me try this." Kelsie hurried over and embedded herself in the group. "We'll all move at once."

Before Marlys could caution Kelsie to be careful, Kelsie used a sweeping motion to encompass the group. They disappeared. For a few seconds, Marlys saw nothing.

"Where'd they go?" Janna said.

"Here!" Kelsie called from the greenhouse door.

"Kelsie," Thorne said sternly. "You shouldn't take chances like that."

"Why? Everything turned out all right."

"What if it hadn't?" Thorne said.

"I can control it," Kelsie said. "I can feel it working."

Marlys turned to Serena. "Can someone feel an artifact working?"

Serena shrugged. "I can feel a sorcerous connection when I use the trident, and when I tracked you with the lance. I suppose that's what she means."

"Let me try to go farther." Kelsie inclined her head and put her hands together, which seemed awkward since one hand still held the hook. "Pleeeeese?" She said, facing Marlys.

"All right," Marlys said. "Just tell me...."

But Kelsie and the apprentices were already gone.

Thorne cast a locator spell. "They're at Valleyview."

"That far?" Celestine said.

Marlys opened a sorcerous channel. "Kelsie, come back here. Now."

"Yes, High Sorcerer Marlys."

Kelsie and the apprentices appeared in front of Marlys. Kelsie detached herself from the group, strode up to Rochelle, and extended the hook with a bow. "Thank you, Sorcerer Rochelle."

Rochelle grasped the proffered hook. "Congratulations on your ascendancy, Sorcerer Kelsie."

Kelsie smiled and rushed back toward the fortress, only to bounce against the barrier. She stepped back, unharmed. The apprentices caught up with her and stopped. Oriana created a gap and let them all back in.

Tir nodded in the direction Kelsie had gone. "An affinity for sorcerous artifacts? A special talent?"

Celestine sighed. "Who knows?"

"I think you underestimated what Kelsie can do," Janna said. When the other sorcerers turned to her, Janna added, "With all due respect." She headed toward the fortress.

Marlys extended a hand and created a gap in the barrier for Janna to pass though.

Rochelle tapped the curve of the hook against a palm. "It's remarkable that Celestine and I tested this artifact and never once thought it could do anything more than move small objects around."

"Sometimes an outside perspective can yield greater results," Serena said.

"Yes," Thorne said. "Remarkable ingenuity. Appalling lack of maturity."

Marlys turned to Voni. "It seems that you have a significant task in front of you."

Voni nodded. "Elspeth was better than I at connecting with Kelsie and teaching her common sense. In Kelsie's case, a sterner approach seems to have had a greater effect. She has made progress."

Thorne snorted. "Some have limits as to how much progress they can make, no matter how much effort is put into it."

Voni turned to Thorne. "Do you want to take over tutoring her?"

"Me?" Thorne said. "You just saw for yourself how effective my warnings were. No, she's better off with you at Valleyview, mostly because of Janna. Janna has the most influence over her, and Janna does try. Not to diminish your effectiveness. I don't think anyone here could do better."

Voni waved a hand. "I understand. No insult taken."

Marlys gestured toward the fortress. "Shall we rejoin the celebration?"

While others went ahead, Serena lingered behind with Marlys. "I think that Thorne is right. Kelsie has an innate talent, but little in the way of self-restraint. I agree with Tir that she needs to be closely supervised. She could be an asset, but she also could be a hazard to herself and others."

"Agreed," Marlys said.

Chapter 13

For some time after Kelsie's ceremony, the strategy of remaining behind barriers seemed to work. Thorne continued to cast the locator spell regularly. Five days later, Argent still had not reappeared.

"He's up to something," Thorne said to Marlys after another failed attempt to find him. They both were in their shared suite. Thorne sat at her desk in the area between their bedrooms. Marlys sat in her room at her own desk. The door between stood open.

"Anything could have happened," Marlys said. "He could be sick. The sorcerers there may have taken him into custody."

Thorne snorted. "I wouldn't count on it."

Marlys heard a knock at the door to the hall, which was also open. Both Marlys and Thorne turned.

Astrid stood at the opening. "May I come in?"

"Of course," Marlys and Thorne said at the same time.

Astrid walked in. "Another night passed without any sign of Argent or his men. However, I heard from other regions that their citizens want to leave the protective barriers and travel on the roads, as usual."

"Do they realize they're risking death?" Thorne said.

Astrid nodded. "They're willing to take the risk."

"We have assigned sorcerers to move things from one location to another by way of transportation and end point spells," Marlys said.

"And we opened the storage units, so everyone is well supplied with food," Thorne added.

"It's more than that," Astrid said. "For instance, the woodcutters can't go out into the forests for logging. The sawmills are idle, which means carpenters and builders aren't able to get lumber. We can move baskets of grain and vegetables through an end point, but we can't transport a cow or a horse, much less an entire herd. We can move animals and carts by way of the distance shortening spell, but that doesn't cover as much of a distance, and we have to be outside the barriers for that to be effective."

Marlys sighed. "I took situations such as that into account, but I thought that citizens would agree that safety was more important."

"Many citizens agree," Astrid said. "Some don't."

"They'll just have to stay where they are," Thorne said.

Astrid tilted her head. "Edwina has reported that some citizens in Briarhill have ventured outside, since it doesn't require sorcery to go through a barrier as long as you were within it when the spell was cast. They've been emboldened by the fact that nothing has happened to them."

"That's because Argent hasn't returned from the island worlds yet," Thorne said. "He doesn't give us advance notice when he will come, and when he does appear, any citizen in his path could die."

"Edwina thinks that there's a way to minimize risk," Astrid said. "She's been in touch with other high sorcerers who are of the same mind. She wanted me to pass on the request to Marlys to use her Library sorcery to talk to all the regions at once this evening. The sorcerers elsewhere will be ready to listen in."

Marlys sighed. "I realized that eventually we would reach a point where tradespeople would be clamoring to go back to their usual routes, but I hoped we would not reach that point until much later."

"I hoped that everyone would wait until Argent was defeated," Thorne said. "We weren't planning to keep everyone confined forever, after all."

"Edwina fears that more citizens will start taking risks and we'll have a catastrophe on our hands," Astrid said.

"She has a point," Marlys said. "If citizens are breaching the barrier at Briarhill, they're probably beginning to sneak out at other locations as well. We have to take the lead on this." She faced Astrid squarely. "You said that they'd be expecting a conference tonight?"

"Yes," Astrid said. "The feeling was that you would accept the request."

Marlys smiled. "It's nice to know that I have the confidence of so many."

"Well earned," Astrid said, returning the smile.

Thorne let out a brief chuckle. "Or it means they're taking you for granted, Marlys."

"I can live with that, too. Better that than no confidence whatsoever."

That evening, well after the food had been cleared from the tables, Marlys sat in the dining hall to open the sorcerous channels. Interested sorcerers and apprentices gathered nearby to watch.

Once Marlys had cast the spell, she was connected with sorcerers from the Library District through the spell passage through the southern regions and numerous points in between.

"I understand," Marlys said, "that citizens have been asking to leave the barriers to travel along their usual trade routes."

She was answered with several affirmations.

"I also understand that Edwina has an idea to address this request," Marlys said.

"Thank you, Marlys," Edwina said. "In discussing this issue with other sorcerers as well as citizens, we have come to some conclusions. Most important, we know there is only one sorcerer to deal with: Argent."

"One is more than enough," Divira said.

"Yes," Edwina agreed. "But he can be only in one place at one time. Right now, he's nowhere on this world. We're constantly casting location spells to be sure of this."

"The problem is, he could reappear anywhere at any time," Ilse said.

"True," Edwina said. "But if each location sends out a willing group at the same time on the same day, at most only one of the groups would be endangered, and even then only if Argent happened to appear at that location."

"In which case, at that location, there could be a disaster," Ilse said.

"Not necessarily," Edwina said. "I propose that sorcerers accompany each group of citizens. If Argent appears, those sorcerers can immediately call upon Marlys. Her fortress has the weapons. They could come to the aid of the threatened party."

"That would not be a guarantee against casualties," Marlys said.

"True, there is risk," Edwina said. "But we have citizens and sorcerers here who would be willing to take that risk. Marlys and the Goldenvalley sorcerers have caused Argent to retreat every time."

"But not the first time," Marlys said. "We were the ones who had to retreat, as you recall."

"That was before you had the sorcerous weapons," Edwina pointed out.

"Sorcerous weapons aren't a guarantee," Ware said. "Elspeth died despite them."

"Besides," Ilse said, "Argent isn't acting alone. He has men with him, and they have charms that make them resistant to most spells."

"Spells, yes," Edwina said. "But not a good hard punch to the gut. Or a knife to the ribs. We found that out at the first encounter. The citizens volunteering to go include magistrate's deputies, trained to fight. According to Rochelle over at Goldenvalley, Argent's fighters don't seem to be experienced in fighting."

"That's true," Rochelle interjected. "But even amateurs can be dangerous."

"Marlys," Edwina said, "one of the citizens here, Cullen, asked for leave to speak to you. May I invite him in?"

"Of course," Marlys said.

Edwina gestured to someone Marlys could not see. She heard heavy footsteps. A man came into view: medium height, short beard, heavily muscled arms showing below his short sleeves. He wore a green vest over a yellow shirt and a green felt cap.

He bowed his head. "Esteemed High Sorcerer."

"I'm interested in what you have to say," Marlys said. "Please proceed."

He raised his head. "I speak for many, esteemed one. We have been attacked. High Sorcerer Edwina tells us that our attacker wishes to rule us. We must show him we will not be subdued."

"We are," Marlys said. "Every sorcerer on this world is dedicated to defeating Argent."

"We wish to join in this effort," Cullen said.

"I don't doubt it," Marlys said. "But you realize that we set up the barriers for your safety."

"For our little ones, yes, our elderly, our vulnerable ones. We understand that you value our lives and we are grateful for your protection. But we feel that it is time for us to act as well."

"Do you realize that Argent has a weapon that, if pointed at you, will instantly result in your death?" Marlys said. "That is how one of our most experienced sorcerers died."

Cullen bowed his head again. "An event that has caused us much sorrow as well." He looked up. "But just as you esteemed sorcerers have taken risk upon yourselves voluntarily, we, too, are prepared to face such risks. We have a plan."

"I'm ready to hear your plan," Marlys said.

"There are elders in Briarhill who remember Argent as a child and youth," Cullen said. "They say that he traveled little. He did not take on an apprenticeship, and showed scant interest in any occupation except thieving. He knows Riverglen because his parents traded here, but he would not know any of the guild lore."

"Such as?" Marlys asked.

"The ancient trade route though Rift Valley," Cullen said.

Thorne frowned. "No one goes there. It's nothing but rocks. The path meanders. The sides are so steep the sun barely shines through the cracks in the ridges. The main roads are faster and straighter."

Cullen nodded. "That is why we think we can take goods through the ridge valley, unnoticed by Argent."

Durand crept over to Marlys. "He's right. I've been through there. It's rough. It's gloomy. But there are no hiding places for an ambush. It's perfect for single travelers or those transporting valuable goods."

Marlys considered for a moment. "You say you have volunteers willing to take the risk?"

"Yes, esteemed one."

Marlys nodded. "Organize your group."

"Already done, esteemed one. We simply await your word."

"Let me speak further with the other sorcerers and we will send word when ready. We still will want to send sorcerers with you."

"That is our hope as well."

Edwina turned to Cullen. "Thank you."

Cullen walked out of view.

Edwina kept her head turned for a time as his footsteps retreated. She faced Marlys again. "We can continue our conversation."

Durand touched Marlys's shoulder. "May I?"

"Of course."

Durand took a seat by Marlys so that the other sorcerers on the channel could see him. "I've traveled the entire continent, eastern shore to western shore. There are many such routes. Guilds and trades know about them. Main roads can be washed out temporarily or buried under landslides. Bridges can collapse. Every one of them knows alternate routes. They're difficult, but they can be traversed. Argent would take only the easiest, most obvious routes, not the hidden ones. This would reduce the risk of traveling considerably."

"I would add," Lumina said from her fortress along the Passage, "that Argent has yet to venture beyond the western parts of Goldenvalley. I think the risk diminishes greatly the farther east one goes."

"He knows the distance shortening spell," Thorne said, "and he can cast an end point spell, but those limit his reach." She nodded at Marlys. "We know he hasn't the power to cast a transportation spell."

No one spoke for a few moments.

"I think this can work," Lindra said.

"So do I," Niquelle said. "Marlys, you have the last word on this. It's the Goldenvalley sorcerers who will have to respond if Argent shows his head. Yours will be the greatest risk."

Marlys searched the faces of the sorcerers surrounding her. All wore determined expressions. Most nodded.

"Tell the tradespeople to organize their expeditions," Marlys said. "They can go when ready."

Chapter 14

Having consulted sorcerers throughout the continent, Marlys then narrowed her communication to Goldenvalley. She found that the citizens in her region had already asked the training centers to organize traveling groups. North of the fortress, near the Looming Mountains, Skye reported that Isador had been approached by woodcutters to resume their work. They were ready to go. In the eastern part of Goldenvalley, Bronwen and Fern told Marlys that herders in their area asked if they could drive livestock to Meadowlands and Woodlands. In the town of Valleyview, metalworkers had been supplied from the mining areas. The smelters had been in Valleyview town when the barriers went up, and now wanted to go home. They had sent word to Voni that they were confident that they could reach their base safely by taking secret paths known to their guilds.

Marlys almost asked why they had not passed these requests on to her before. After a few moments of thought, she realized that with everyone mourning Elspeth and then celebrating Kelsie's ascension, the subject had not been foremost in their minds the past several days.

"If they're mindful of the danger involved," Marlys said, "and you can find at least two willing sorcerers to go with each group, there's no reason they can't travel when ready. But don't let anyone out without a plan and precautions, and warn the citizens in your areas not to leave the barriers by themselves."

All the Goldenvalley training centers agreed to this.

Marlys closed the channels.

At breakfast the next morning, Astrid reported that groups throughout the continent had begun journeying an hour after sunrise. Everyone at the breakfast table appeared relieved that the traveling parties experienced a peaceful start. When the sorcerers and apprentices had finished eating, and the apprentices began to clean up, Marlys asked the sorcerers to remain.

"Now that road travel has resumed, we will be summoned in the event that Argent shows up. We need a plan."

"I've been thinking that over as well," Serena said.

"I certainly hope the plan for me has not changed," Thorne said. "I take the chest protector and the mace to attack Argent directly."

Rochelle turned to Thorne. "The chest protector, yes. But with him holding that shield, the mace isn't going to do you any good."

"I can still smash his head in with it," Thorne said, "and I can deal with anyone who stands between me and him."

"You can deal with anyone in the way," Rochelle said, "and that may be of use, but a protective spell will stop you from hitting Argent himself with the mace."

"He has such confidence in that shield that I doubt that he'd remember to cast that spell," Thorne said.

"If so, he could still use the shield to deflect the mace," Rochelle said. "It has a physical presence besides being able to ward off spells and spelled weapons."

"Thorne can still draw his attention," Zaria said. "That means he won't be looking for an attack from elsewhere. I've been practicing with Rochelle and I think I can be more accurate with a crossbow next time."

"A crossbow would still be stopped if he remembers to cast a protective spell," Tir said.

"Marlys or I can cancel any protective spell," Serena said. "He won't be able to detect that."

"Yes," Rochelle said, "two attacking him at the same time could be effective."

"Three," Serena said. "If Thorne will allow me to take the strength belt, I have a plan, too. Thorne doesn't need it to distract him."

Thorne turned to Serena. "That's true, but why do you need the strength belt?"

"My plan," Serena said, "is to cast a transportation spell to emerge behind him and wrench the battle axe from his hands."

Tir grinned. "That's a bold move. I like it."

"Make sure you cast a protective spell in case Zaria misses her shot," Rochelle said.

"I endorse that," Zaria added. "Argent could move at the last instant and avoid the bolt."

"Don't worry, I have planned to use all the protective magic I can conjure," Serena said.

"Those are sound plans for confronting Argent," Marlys said. "We also need to think about the civilians. If we are called, it will be because a group traveling on the road is threatened. They will have animals, carts with supplies. We need to protect them, too."

"Argent is the primary danger," Rochelle said. "Stopping him, as I see it, is therefore our primary function."

"I agree," Marlys said. "But he will undoubtedly have men with him. While they can't cause the kind of damage that Argent is capable of, they can still kill and injure."

"The civilians on the trade routes will be armed and ready to fight," Rochelle said.

Marlys nodded. "But I still want to avoid as much bloodshed as possible. I was thinking that the sorcerous hook could be employed to whisk them away."

Rochelle turned to Marlys sharply. "All of them? Marlys, we may be talking about a dozen civilians at least, not to mention the animals and carts."

"Kelsie showed us that the hook can be used to transport multiple people a fair distance," Marlys said. "Perhaps with practice, she could do even more."

"Kelsie?" Rochelle said.

"You aren't seriously thinking of employing Kelsie for something as serious as this?" Thorne said.

"She does seem to have an affinity for that particular artifact," Serena said.

"She's completely unpredictable," Thorne said. "She would be more of a risk than an asset."

"She'd have to be closely watched," Tir said.

"Yes, she'd have to be under strict supervision," Marlys said. "But if she can do it, this will give us an advantage."

"Why not then use the hook to move everyone—civilians, animals, and all—from one town to another and avoid traveling entirely?" Thorne said.

Rochelle raised a finger. "Now that would be worthwhile."

Thorne snorted. "She's entirely undisciplined."

"She can learn," Marlys said. "She's eager to use her sorcery, and I think she would be highly motivated if we gave her a task that she can excel in."

Thorne sighed and shook her head.

Celestine tapped the table thoughtfully. "I think Marlys has a point."

"But we have to make more than one plan in case Kelsie fails," Rochelle said.

"Of course," Marlys said.

"What we've done seems to be working," Tir said. "The hammer has caused Argent's men to flee in panic. The trident still can corral them and keep them from attacking others."

"If Rochelle and Serena can instruct us," Durand said, "the rest of us can take up the remaining weapons and use them as needed."

Rochelle and Serena nodded.

"It seems we have a strategy," Marlys said. "Let's start working on it. I'll take the hook and go to Valleyview while the rest of you practice here."

"You're not bringing Kelsie to the fortress?" Rochelle asked.

"No," Marlys said. "I think Kelsie would be more pliable in surroundings familiar to her."

"I agree," Throne said. "I will go to Valleyview with you."

"Besides," Tir said, "Kelsie might be distracted by the temptation to watch the rest of us handle the other weapons."

"Something that we greatly want to avoid," Thorne said.

While Celestine gathered the apprentices and led them to the fortress's classroom for their regular instruction, Rochelle and Serena selected weapons from the armory. Artifacts in hand, the two sorcerers led a group of interested parties outdoors for instruction in the use of the artifacts.

Marlys and Thorne remained inside. Marlys stood by as Thorne cast yet another locator spell.

"No Argent," she reported.

Marlys nodded. "I'm going to check on the Goldenvalley companies." Opening a sorcerous channel, she contacted Skye first.

"Have you reached the forest?" Marlys asked.

"Yes. No problems here," Skye reported. "The woodcutters are plying their trade. We have horse-drawn sledges ready to transport the logs to the nearest sawmill through a little-known route. I'm planning on using the distance shortening spell as much as I can."

"Good," Marlys said.

"I'm casting the locator spell for Argent regularly," Skye added.

"So are we," Marlys said. "We haven't detected as much as a hint of him."

"Let's hope it stays that way," Skye said, "at least until everyone has reached their destination."

"That is my wish as well," Marlys said. "May the Bright Beings watch over you."

"You also."

Marlys closed the connection and opened a channel to Bronwen. "Are the herders on their way?"

"Yes, I'm on horseback with the leaders," Bronwen said. "Fern is back at the training center. Ivy is with us at the end of the line. I'm about to cast a distance shortening spell to speed us on our way."

"Sounds as if all is well there," Marlys said. "May the Bright Beings guide your path."

"Yours too."

Marlys closed the channel and opened one to Voni. "Have the smelters left for home?"

"Yes," Voni said. "Freida and Hazel volunteered to go with them. They're already well on their way."

"Good," Marlys said. "I also called to say that Thorne and I would like to go there to help Kelsie get more practice with the use of the hook."

Before Voni could respond, Marlys heard rapid footsteps and Kelsie's voice saying, "Yes! Yes! Yes! Yes! Yes!" as she came into view. She leaned against Voni and grinned at Marlys.

Marlys almost asked why Kelsie was not in class before remembering Kelsie was a sorcerer now and would be receiving instructions from more experienced sorcerers.

Voni turned to Kelsie, smiled, and gave Kelsie a one-armed hug. Facing Marlys again, she said, "You are welcome to come whenever you're ready."

"We'll be there soon." Marlys closed the channel. She walked over to the armory wall and removed the hook. "Shall we go?" she said to Thorne.

Thorne nodded.

Marlys cast a transportation spell. They stepped through and appeared at Valleyview, just outside the barrier.

The door of the training center opened. Kelsie made an opening in the barrier and ran toward Marlys and Thorne. She embraced Thorne. Before Thorne could respond, Kelsie embraced Marlys, which proved somewhat awkward with Marlys holding the hook.

Kelsie released Marlys, stepped back, and smiled. "I'm ready!"

By that time, other sorcerers and apprentices had joined them.

Thorne put a hand on Kelsie's shoulder and looked her in the eye. "Can you follow instructions this time?"

"Oh, yes!" Kelsie said enthusiastically.

"You're going to test her ability to use the weapon?" Janna asked.

"That's the idea," Marlys said.

"I'll do anything to get rid of Argent," Kelsie said.

"You're not going to do that, at least not directly," Marlys said.

Kelsie's brow furrowed.

"There are groups of tradespeople already on the road," Marlys said. "We need to be prepared in the event that Argent shows up with his men and they call Goldenvalley for help."

"The experienced sorcerers," Thorne explained, "are the ones who will take action against Argent himself. We hope that you can use the hook to move the civilians out of the way so the rest of us can attack him."

Voni took a step toward Kelsie. "This is very important work. They're asking you to do it because they think no one else could do it better."

Kelsie's eyebrows and pressed lips moved, indicating, Marlys hoped, she was thinking it over. Then her expression brightened. "I'll do it!"

"Good." Marlys looked around. Nearly all of Valleyview's sorcerers and apprentices had joined them. The sky was clear, the weather warm, the breeze moderate. Gesturing, Marlys added,

"Let's step over to the main road. If the rest of you are willing, you can pretend to be civilians that Kelsie can practice moving with the hook." She started walking in that direction. Behind her, she heard the apprentices chattering excitedly. Glancing back, she saw sorcerers following with interested expressions.

The cobblestone road lay empty in both directions, as Marlys had expected. To the east, she could see roofs of the taller buildings of Valleyview town above the treetops.

Marlys waved at a group of apprentices. "Stand in a line on the road."

They lined up as instructed.

Marlys turned to Kelsie. "If Argent and his men attack, the civilians may or may not be together. I want to see if you can use the hook to snag every other apprentice and move them just a few paces down the road."

"I can move them farther," Kelsie said.

"We'll get to that," Marlys assured her. "Right now, I just want to see if you can separate the civilians from the attackers." He handed Kelsie the hook.

Kelsie took it, adjusted the grip in both hands, and proceeded to move it. Every other apprentice disappeared. Kelsie moved the hook westward and the apprentices reappeared when Kelsie stopped moving.

"Excellent." Marlys gestured to the relocated apprentices. "Come on back."

As they rejoined the group, Voni turned to Marlys. "How will Kelsie distinguish a civilian from Argent's men?"

"The clothing is remarkably different," Thorne said. "Argent's men all look as if they're wearing oversized garments. The fabrics look as if the dyers splashed bright colors on them and the clothing is crudely sewn. Besides, they all wear the same charm that Janna retrieved."

Marlys addressed the apprentices again. "Probably no one will be standing still. I want you to walk around, back and forth and in circles."

"Like a dance?" an apprentice asked.

"That will do," Marlys said. "Clasp hands, too, because some attackers may place hands on our civilians."

The apprentices obeyed.

"Kelsie," Marlys said, "pick any three from among the group and move them as far as you did before."

This time Kelsie adjusted her two-handed grip on the hook. She surveyed the group and adjusted her grip again. Just as Marlys thought Kelsie might be giving up, Kelsie took a deep breath, wove the hook from side to side, gathered the apprentices and moved them.

"Now that," Thorne said as the apprentices came back, "was impressive."

Marlys gestured to the remaining spectators. "Everyone get on the road. Remember to circulate among yourselves." When they had done so, she turned to Kelsie. "Pick out the sorcerers and relocate them."

With a determined expression, Kelsie again worked the hook and accomplished the task.

"Congratulations, Kelsie," Voni said as she walked toward Marlys.

Kelsie beamed with pride.

"The civilians will have carts and animals with them," Marlys said. "Can some of you go to the barn and bring out a cart and horse?"

Three of the apprentices ran.

"Marlys," Voni said, "isn't that stretching things a bit? I think moving people around will be more than sufficient."

"Yes, if Kelsie can't do it, moving people around will be enough," Marlys said. "But I want to see if she can do it."

"So do I!" Kelsie said.

Voni shrugged and sighed.

After a time, the apprentices came back. One led a cow. Another led a goat. The third led a horse drawing a cart.

When they had reached the road and mingled with the others, Marlys said to Kelsie, "This time, move the apprentices and animals only. Again, just a small distance away."

After taking deep breaths and manipulating the hook, Kelsie started moving the hook. Apprentices, animals, and cart disappeared and reappeared down the road. The animals seemed calm and unfazed by the change in location.

"Excellent, Kelsie," Marlys said. "Now we can see if you can move everyone farther."

"What did you have in mind?" Thorne asked.

"The Valleyview town square should be sufficient," Marlys said. "Would you mind going there and making sure it's empty?"

"Certainly." Thorne cast an end point spell and disappeared.

Meanwhile, everyone assembled on the road in front of Marlys again.

Thorne appeared through the sorcerous channels. "The town square is empty."

"Can you bring the apprentices and animals there?" Marlys asked Kelsie.

"Oh, yes," Kelsie said enthusiastically. She squared her shoulders and manipulated the hook. Only the sorcerers remained.

"They're here," Thorne said.

Marlys turned to Kelsie. "Now bring them back."

Kelsie's eyebrows went up, as if she had not been expecting the request. But she lifted the artifact and everyone, including Thorne, appeared again.

"That was extraordinary," Marlys said. "Thank you."

Kelsie's shoulders slumped. "That's all I can do right now. I'm tired."

Marlys reached over and put a hand on Kelsie's shoulder. "That's all you need to do for the moment. I'll take the hook again."

Kelsie returned it to Marlys.

"Surely you knew that an extended use of magic can wear one out," Thorne said, "especially if you're not used to doing so."

Kelsie answered with a weak smile and a small shrug.

Marlys put a hand on Kelsie's shoulder. "We're all proud of you, Kelsie. We'll call on you if we need you."

Voni turned to the Valleyview assembly. "Thank you. You can return to what you were doing."

The apprentices who had brought out the animals returned them to the barn. Others opened the barrier to go back inside the building.

Janna put an arm around Kelsie's shoulder. "See? I told you it would be worth it to become a sorcerer."

Kelsie smiled. "It's fun, but it's a lot of work."

Janna grinned. "You'll get used to it. Come, let's join the others."

When they had gone, Voni faced Marlys and Thorne. "Anything else?"

"No, we'll get back to the fortress," Marlys said. "Thank you again for your hospitality."

"Come any time." Voni waved a goodbye and returned to the building.

"Let's hope that once Kelsie is rested, she won't be pestering us to use the hook," Thorne said.

"She can't enter the fortress without our opening the barrier there," Marlys said. "She can't sneak in and get it."

"No, but now that she can use the sorcerous channels, we may be hearing from her often."

Marlys sighed. "This is the least of our problems right now. Let's hope that Voni and Janna can urge some restraint."

"I hope so. I'm not counting on it, however."

Chapter 15

When Marlys and Thorne returned to the fortress, they found Serena and Rochelle outside instructing the other sorcerers. Nessa had the trident and was in the process of encircling a group of five. They stood together shoulder to shoulder, and their pressing against the perimeter described by the trident failed to breach it.

"Good work," Rochelle said to Nessa.

"How do I turn it off?" Nessa asked.

"Just lift it and aim it at the sky," Rochelle said.

Nessa rotated the trident so that the three prongs pointed upward.

The sorcerers found they could move again and separated.

Serena turned to Marlys. "How well did Kelsie handle the hook?"

"She was able to snag designated people, along with a cart and three animals, and move them as far as Valleyview town," Marlys said.

"That's impressive," Rochelle said. "Maybe she can just move tradespeople and their goods from town to town so that the processions won't be necessary."

Thorne shook her head. "The effort exhausted her. She needs to stay fresh so that she can help us defeat Argent. Constant use of the hook would drain her completely."

"Perhaps others could learn to use it?" Durand asked.

"None of us have been able to do more than move one person from here to there," Rochelle said.

Marlys held the hook out. "You're welcome to try if you wish."

Durand grasped the hook. He motioned to three sorcerers to stand at a distance. Aiming the hook at them, he attempted to move them, but nothing happened.

Other sorcerers took a turn, and also failed.

"There's no reason to feel defeated," Serena told them. "Rochelle and I couldn't do more than relocate each other."

"Maybe it's similar to the speed reading spell, which only you and I and Blair can do," Nessa said.

"Not every sorcerer can perform every spell," Thorne said. "We all have our special talents."

"Then we can feel grateful that Kelsie can help us," Durand said.

"Absolutely," Marlys said.

Two days later, Marlys was taking a quiet moment in the kitchen. She had just taken a sip of tea when Thorne entered the room.

"I just cast a locator spell. Argent has returned to this world," Thorne said.

Before Marlys could respond, Kelsie's image appeared. "We found Argent. I'm ready!"

Thorne sighed and shook her head slightly.

"I'm delighted that you're prepared to help," Marlys said. "But we must find out what he's up to first. If he's not attacking anyone, Thorne and Serena and I will simply observe him for a time."

Kelsie's face fell.

Voni's image joined Kelsie's. "Kelsie, Marlys will tell us when you are needed. Meanwhile, you need to keep on learning and practicing the spells that Janna and I are teaching you."

"Voni's right," Marlys said. "The more spells you know, the more you'll be able to help when the time comes."

Kelsie's frown changed to a weak smile.

"Now, show me that you can close a sorcerous channel, too," Voni said.

Kelsie's and Voni's images faded.

Thorne clicked her tongue. "Impatient."

Marlys placed her cup and saucer on the counter and quickly cleaned them sorcerously. "She's enthusiastic. She'll learn." She headed toward the kitchen door.

"That's optimistic," Thorne said, following Marlys.

When Marlys and Thorne reached the armory wall, they found Serena already there. "Same plan as last time?"

"Yes," Marlys said.

Thorne moved to the wall map and pointed. "He's here, by the entrance to the underground chambers. We can observe from the hilltop here."

Marlys grabbed the trident, vambrace, and lance. Thorne put on the chest protector and removed the mace from the wall. Serena wrapped the belt around her and took the trident and one of the stakes.

"Ready?" Marlys said. When they nodded, she cast the transportation spell.

They emerged in a wooded area overlooking the entrance to the underground residence. Marlys made sure they had cast concealing spells before stepping out from the trees into a clearing. Serena used the stake to set a protective perimeter.

Though Marlys could see the area well, she cast a far-seeing spell to catch more details. Argent stood to one side, shield on one arm, battle axe held in the other hand.

"He has a hook on his belt," Thorne observed.

Marlys nodded. "I saw that."

"I wonder if he knows how to use it," Thorne said.

"He's had time to practice," Marlys said.

"Look at all the supplies, the packs, the baskets," Serena said. "I've counted 37 men so far, and more may be already underground. Before, he had only a dozen or so men with him, 20 at most."

"It seems this is a staging area," Marlys said. "They're moving the supplies underground."

"They're planning to be here a while," Thorne said.

"Gathering an army?" Serena said.

"He intends to conquer," Thorne said, "and he's mentioned before that he needed more men."

"I'm seeing weapons," Marlys said. "Short swords, knives, spears, bows and arrows."

"Argent just seems to be walking around," Serena said. "I don't see his lips moving, and there isn't much sound from the men, either."

"I'll aim the lance and see if I can catch anything." Marlys lifted the lance and pointed it toward Argent. After a few minutes of silence, she put it down again. "Nothing."

Thorne turned to Marlys. "I don't think we'll learn any more standing here. If he moves significantly from this spot, we'll know it. Sorcerers all over the continent are constantly casting locator spells, not just me."

"We could send someone here every once in a while to confirm whether anything's changed," Serena said.

Marlys nodded. "I think you're both right. Let's return to the fortress."

Once back at the fortress, Marlys found herself surrounded by sorcerers and apprentices with questioning looks.

"Well?" Rochelle said as Marlys, Thorne and Serena put their weapons back on the armory wall.

"He has more men with him this time. They seem to be setting up a base in that underground chamber we were at before," Marlys said.

"They have weapons with them, too," Thorne said.

"What are they planning to do, wave them around?" Zaria said. "They can't breach our protective barriers."

"They know we can't stay within them forever," Thorne said. "We're all essentially under siege, and sieges have limited effectiveness."

"If they find the tradesmen that have been going out," Rochelle said. "They can attack and loot them. Or take hostages."

"Lyra's on watch this afternoon." Marlys amplified her voice. "Lyra?"

"Coming," they heard.

When Lyra appeared, Marlys said, "What's the news about the groups sent out earlier?"

"All safe so far," Lyra said. "The woodcutters have made their quota and delivered the logs to the sawmills. The herders have reached their destinations and are on their way back. The smelters are home and plan to gather more goods and start their usual rounds. Cullen's party has passed the borders of Cloverdell without incident."

"I'm worried about citizens going past the barrier on their own without a plan," Durand said, "and without sorcerers accompanying them to alert us."

"So am I," Marlys said. "The fact that tradespeople have ventured out and returned safely may embolden some to take risks."

"And we'll have no warning of that," Thorne said.

Marlys turned to Lyra. "Send word to the others to do their best to prevent anyone stepping out from the barriers without authorization. The magistrates may have to organize citizen patrols to make sure that no one leaves secretly."

Lyra nodded and left.

"While Argent is occupied here," Marlys said, "and I suspect he'll be here for a long time, I want to go back to the island worlds and investigate the 'treasures' the obelisk told me about." She looked over at the apprentices. "Oriana, would you get me a carry bag?"

Oriana nodded and hurried away.

"Bringing treasures back?" Tir asked.

"If I find them," Marlys said. "Better with us than sitting in the obelisk."

"They could prove dangerous to remove," Rochelle said.

"The voice seemed to be making an offer," Marlys said, "like the voices were heard at Overlook."

"'Use them wisely,'" Tir quoted. "That seems to indicate an expectation that the treasures would be accessed."

"Exactly," Marlys said. Oriana brought back a carry bag and gave it to Marlys. Marlys shouldered it. "Thank you."

Oriana smiled and stepped back.

"This time, I'm going with you," Serena said. "Someone has to read the spell book."

"I can read it," Nessa said.

"True," Serena said, "but Marlys needs someone who's experienced in uncovering any secret or hidden writing, according to what she told us about it."

"Come back as quickly as you can," Durand said. "I wouldn't want to be without you both if there's a crisis."

Marlys heard sounds of agreement from the others. "I expect to be home by the evening meal."

"We'll be waiting," Tir said.

"May the Bright Beings watch over you," Celestine said.

Marlys and Serena walked out beyond the protective barrier. Once Marlys opened the portal to the island worlds, they stepped through.

Marlys immediately looked around. As before, no one was in sight.

Serena turned around. "The portal closed quickly once we were through. It's amazingly calm on this side."

"I felt the same."

Serena cast a bordering spell. "It's fortunate that we're out of sight of anyone. The road curves, the trees and the grain block the view on one side, the house blocks the view on the other, and the remaining space is occupied only by cattle. We'll hear a warning if anyone comes close."

Marlys nodded and faced the manor house.

"Allow me." Serena cast a spell. "The revealing spell tells me no one's home."

"Good. Let's get busy with the obelisk." Marlys moved toward the base. She pulled out the drawer and the seat. "Here's the spell book."

Serena sat. "It's open to the page which lists the sorcerous artifacts here, including the hook. Presumably that was what he most recently searched for."

Marlys nodded. "I'll see if I can find whatever else the obelisk has to offer." Taking a step back, she looked up and cast her most powerful spell toward it. The ladder carving lit up.

"Welcome, sorcerer."

Serena lifted her head. "You seem to have its attention."

"There are many treasures within to uncover," the voice continued. "Use them wisely."

"That's the problem with spelling items to talk," Marlys said. "It's the same words every time."

"It's glowing sorcerously," Serena said. "You must have activated something."

"I'll conceal myself and use the climbing spell to see if I can find a hidden compartment farther up," Marlys said.

"I'll keep reading," Serena said.

Once concealed, Marlys cast the climbing spell and began to ascend. When she reached a level even with the top of the manor house, she looked around. Below her and to one side, the ditch showed signs of recent digging. *Probably where Argent's men unearthed the hook*, she thought. Turning her attention toward the road and beyond, she saw no sign of anyone coming in her direction.

She let out a sigh of relief and turned to the obelisk. The ladder indentations on one side of the obelisk glowed, as they had before. She found more indentations on other faces, at her level and above. If they were symbols or letters, they were none she recognized.

Placing the fingers on her right hand together, she pressed a straight indentation. A panel slid back. Peering inside the space, she saw a shiny black square.

"A mirror," the obelisk voice explained. "To reflect a spell upon its caster."

Marlys reached in and grasped it by an edge. Cautiously, she removed the square. She met no resistance, and nothing happened when she pulled it out. Turning it over, she found a loop in the back, enabling her to hold it firmly. When she examined the shiny side, she saw a perfect reflection of herself.

Although the mirror seemed solidly made, not fragile at all, she carefully slid it into the carry bag. When she faced the obelisk again, the panel had slid shut by itself.

"Make sure to get the sentinel stone," Serena called.

Marlys looked down to see Serena looking up at her. Either Serena knew a spell to observe someone concealed or she had guessed Marlys's general location from hearing the obelisk's voice.

"I found the page with the list of obelisk treasures," Serena said. "The letters nearly faded to invisibility. I had to cast a spell of power to reveal them."

Marlys craned her neck upward, examining the indentations above her. "There's no indication where a sentinel stone might be."

"There aren't any descriptions in the book as to where they are either. Only the list."

"I have a mirror."

Serena consulted the book. "I thought you would retrieve it after the voice spoke. The mirror would be useful. Any or all of them could help us. Some more than others."

"How many?"

"Ten listed. That doesn't mean that's all of them, though. Artifacts could be hidden in the obelisk that no one listed."

"What else did you read about besides the mirror and sentinel stone?"

"A lantern for light, a silvery round platter for spying, a scythe for harvesting, a flute for wind, a crystal for cold, a disc with a sun painted on it for warmth, a prism for rain, and a cracked vase for dryness."

Marlys felt her sack. "I don't think I have room for them all."

"Neither do I, even though the book says all of them are lightweight and can be held in one hand. We'll have to take what we can and be satisfied that at least Argent doesn't have the sorcerous power to retrieve them or use them."

"What would you recommend?"

"Besides the mirror and the sentinel stone? Take the platter, the flute, and the prism. Those would be the most use against Argent."

"I'll find them. Keep reading."

Serena nodded.

Marlys reached up to the next indentation she saw. Placing her fingers in it, she pressed gently. Nothing happened. Using more force did not produce results, either. Perhaps some of the indentations were simply decorative.

She propelled herself up a little more and pressed the next indentation. This time a panel opened to reveal a shiny round platter.

"To look into. See and hear from far away," the voice said.

Marlys removed the platter and gently slipped it into the carry bag next to the mirror.

By progressing slowly, testing the indentations, and listening to the voices, Marlys gathered the sentinel stone, the prism, and the flute. By that time, she had reached the pointed top of the obelisk.

Looking out, taking in the view, she could again see people traveling up and down the road. Some walked alone, some walked in groups, some drove carts of various sizes. Most of the activity was close to towns, and to the city on the horizon. Elsewhere, herders tended to cattle, farmers harvested crops, people drew water from wells, and children played in clearings. No one, however, seemed interested in heading in her direction, which was a relief and a curiosity. Perhaps Argent had a bad reputation and no one wanted to come near?

Slowly, carefully, Marlys climbed down her invisible sorcerous ladder until she reached the ground.

Serena met her there and gestured to the bag. "May I see?"

Marlys slid the bag off her shoulder and handed it to Serena. "Of course."

Serena sat and rummaged through the bag, taking out each artifact and examining it closely before returning it.

"Were you able to read the entire spell book?" Marlys asked.

Serena faced her and smiled. "Yes, even the hidden text."

"Anything interesting?"

"Interesting but not necessarily useful." She waved at the area around them. "Apparently, when sorcerers send people here from our world, they all land in this vicinity. Historically, some have stayed here and settled down. It seems those on the losing side of the sorcerous wars did. They were exhausted after the fight, and the sorcerers from the city made it plain they were not going to tolerate hostilities. They built the manor house and the obelisk, stored their most valuable and powerful artifacts in it and buried the others. After that, they lived long lives of quiet prosperity, using sorcery to gain allies and generate wealth."

Marlys nodded. "Their sorcery would greatly enhance their ability to mine, harvest, and craft goods as well as to transport them."

"Through the centuries, the others we sent here had various outcomes. All, it seems, were prevented from wreaking havoc anywhere beyond this particular province. Some stayed here, some traveled elsewhere. A few, it seems, even went to the capital and joined the ruling sorcerers there."

"Recorded in the book?"

Serena turned to the open book. "I doubt that every one of them wrote something. Most of the writing was from the fugitives of the sorcerous wars from our world. Occasionally I saw writing from different hands. Probably every once in a while, someone felt it important to return here and add to the record." She stood and handed the bag back to Marlys. "I left the book open at the page where we found it. Argent, if and when he returns, should have no sign that we were here."

Marlys pushed back the seat and the drawer. She faced Serena. "Ready to go home?"

"For now. We can return if we need to."

"Let's cast the spell then," Marlys said.

"Trap spell within end point spell," Serena recited. "Pull the lever and activate the star."

Marlys did so. A portal opened immediately.

Serena smiled at Marlys. "If only defeating Argent were so easily done."

"One challenge at a time," Marlys said, as they both stepped through to their own world.

Chapter 16

Marlys and Serena returned to their own world at a point just outside the protective barrier around the Goldenvalley fortress. The portal closed behind them once they stepped on solid ground.

They passed the barrier and walked to the empty audience room. The door to the dining hall stood open. Marlys could hear the sounds of low conversation and smelled roast chicken.

"Evening meal," Serena said.

Marlys nodded. Pulling the strap on her bag she carried higher on her shoulder, she walked into the hall with Serena. As she strode to a place with empty seats, she heard, "Welcome back!" "How did it go?" "What did you find?"

"We'll be happy to answer questions once we're settled," Marlys said.

They took places at a table. Marlys put her bag underneath the seat. Immediately, Oriana rose and brought them plates, utensils, and mugs. Others at the table passed them platters and pitchers.

As Marlys and Serena served themselves, Tir said, "I see you brought something back. The bag looked full."

"Treasures," Marlys said between bites.

"Among them," Serena said, "we brought back a mirror to reflect spells, a sentinel stone to signal someone approaching, a platter to use to spy on someone, a flute to produce wind, and a prism to generate rain."

"There were others," Marlys added, "but we didn't have the means to carry them all."

"Everything you listed will be useful," Thorne said. "Too bad you couldn't have brought back more."

"We have what we need, I think," Marlys said.

"Besides, we can return later if we need more," Serena said.

"What about the spell book?" Tir asked.

"I read all of it," Serena said, "including all the hidden text."

"Naturally there would be hidden text," Thorne said dryly.

"Anything of tactical advantage?" Rochelle asked.

Serena shook her head. "There were several killing spells recorded, all of which we know already. But now we can be sure that Argent knows them."

"All he needs is that battle axe," Thorne said.

"Which I plan to relieve him of at the first opportunity," Serena said.

Marlys looked around. "And what have you been doing while we were away?"

"Weapons training," Tir said. "We paused to eat."

"Has Argent moved?" Marlys asked.

"No," Thorne said.

"As soon as I'm done eating," Serena said, "I'm going to the roof of the fortress to set up the sentinel stone. It will alert us if anyone approaches the fortress."

"Alert how?" Durand asked.

"Sorcerous chime," Serena said.

Thorne sighed. "I hope it's not too loud. It'll give us all a headache otherwise."

"According to the description," Serena said, "it's loud enough to be heard but low enough not to be painful to the ear."

When they had finished eating, Serena took the sentinel stone out of the bag. It was about the width of her hand, rounded, smooth, and translucent.

"Mind if I join you?" Nessa asked.

"Not at all," Serena said, and walked out with her.

Celestine assumed the supervision of the kitchen duty.

The remainder of the sorcerers went to the armory and removed artifacts from the wall. Marlys had slung the carry bag over a shoulder again.

"Marlys, you should practice with some of these, too," Rochelle said.

"I'm interested in seeing if I can use the hook and the trident," Marlys said. "Those seem to require a certain amount of finesse."

"I'm interested in trying the artifacts you brought back," Zaria said. Other sorcerers nodded in agreement.

"Let's wait for Serena to return before trying those," Marlys said. "She's the one who read the instructions. Meanwhile, we can try out the other artifacts."

Rochelle led the way outside, opened the barrier, and closed it after everyone walked through. Marlys put the bag down in a grassy area and gestured at Rochelle to pass her the hook.

"Let's see if I can use this," Marlys said.

Tir raised a hand and walked to the clearing. "I'll volunteer to let you move me."

When Tir stopped and faced her, Marlys pointed the hook at him. He disappeared. She moved the hook in a half circle. Tir reappeared at the place Marlys pointed to when she stopped.

"Can you move more than one person?" Rochelle said.

"Let's see," Marlys said.

Without prompting, Zaria and Durand strode toward Tir. When they stopped, Marlys tried to snag them all with the hook, and failed.

She sighed, faced Rochelle, and extended the hook. "Seems I can't."

Rochelle grasped the hook. "None of the rest of us could, either."

Marlys extended a hand to Thorne, who held the trident, points up. "Let me see what I can do with this."

Manipulating the trident, Marlys performed a lassoing motion in the direction of the group of sorcerers. Tir and the others tried to break out of the perimeter but could not. Marlys moved the trident to one side and found the sorcerers were obliged to move with it.

Marlys pointed the trident upwards again, releasing the sorcerers.

"Not bad," Tir said as he walked toward Marlys.

Serena and Nessa emerged from the fortress.

"The sentinel stone is in place," Serena said.

"Good," Marlys said. "We were waiting for you before trying out the treasures."

Tir extended his hand. "May I try the mirror?"

"Of course." Marlys removed it from the bag and handed it to him.

Tir grasped the handhold on the mirror and held it in front of him. "I presume the shiny side goes outward."

Durand moved to a place a few paces away and faced Tir. "Let me try a light push spell."

Tir braced himself and raised the mirror. "Go ahead."

Durand cast a pushing spell. Almost immediately, he fell backwards and landed on the seat of his pants. He scrambled to his feet and brushed himself off. "That worked."

Tir took off the mirror. "I felt only a slight pressure." He handed it back to Marlys to put back in the bag.

"I'm curious as to how the flute works." Serena drew it out of the bag.

"Look into it and make sure it's clean before using it," Nessa advised.

Serena did so, saying, "The spell book said it was self-cleaning, but it's prudent to check...it's clean."

"How much of a musician do you have to be to use it?" Thorne asked.

"The book stated it will play its own tune," Serena said. "All I need to do is blow into it." She surveyed the clearing. "Everyone stay behind me." She put the flute to her lips and blew softly. They could see and hear the leaves rustling in the trees beyond the clearing. The flute emitted a high-pitched but pleasant tune. She blew harder and the thinner branches swayed as the tune quickened in tempo. Taking a deep breath, she blew with all her might. Entire trees, trunks and all, bent with the force. The tune this time reminded Marlys of a bugle's wake-up call.

"That's impressive," Tir said.

Serena smiled and took another breath. Blowing moderately, she moved the flute back and forth as she blew it. The wind covered an area defined by the sweep of the flute.

"Definitely worth keeping," Rochelle said.

"Can I try the platter?" Thorne said.

Serena placed the flute back in the bag, brought out the platter, and handed it to Thorne. "Cast a locator spell while holding it and you should be able to spy on whoever you sought out."

"Can whoever I locate see or hear me?" Thorne said.

"No," Serena said. "The viewer can see and hear but the one seen will have no knowledge of being observed."

Thorne smiled. "Good!"

The other sorcerers crowded behind Thorne as she cast the locator spell. Marlys, standing next to Thorne, saw Argent sitting at a table, eating. His plate held roast meat and assorted vegetables. After cutting a piece of meat, chewing, and swallowing, he lifted a mug by his plate and drank.

"More ale!" he called.

Grady came into view with a pitcher and refilled the mug.

The image on the platter faded.

Marlys frowned. "How long is the image supposed to last?"

"The spell book said it would only last a brief time," Serena said.

"Then what use is it?" Thorne handed the platter to Marlys. "We didn't learn anything."

"What use is it?" Rochelle said. "That's far more information than we could get from a locator spell, and we don't have to be in proximity to the subject for the spell to activate, as we have to with the lance. This is a valuable artifact."

"The spell book said the effect only lasts a brief time," Serena said.

"And in that brief time," Rochelle said, "we learned he is still underground, that the underground chambers have room for a dining hall, that they are supplied with ample food, plates and utensils, and most of all, that Argent drinks intoxicating beverages."

"Very unwise," Durand said. "I know of only a few sorcerers who imbibe, and they only take a few sips on rare occasions. Intoxicants blunt the powers."

"True," Rochelle said, "I take a sip of rum now and then, and Celestine does, too, but nothing beyond that."

"I wouldn't even taste it," Thorne said.

"I have had a small cordial of wine in the past myself," Durand said, "but I wouldn't gulp a mug's worth, much less more."

"Probably Argent's men are so afraid of him, they don't even notice how ale affects him," Marlys said. "But it might explain why we haven't detected a protective spell around him when we've confronted him in the past."

"Could his sorcery be immune to the effects of the ale?" Tir mused.

Serena shrugged. "Anything's possible, though I've never heard of such a thing happening. I suspect that Marlys is right. Besides, he has the magical artifacts, and they wouldn't be less potent even if his magic was."

"But one still has to be sorcerer to wield such an artifact," Tir said.

"Drunk or sober, he remains a sorcerer," Thorne said. "Ale would diminish his powers, not cancel them."

"It is too bad that we can't use it to keep a constant watch on Argent, though," Tir said.

"We use what we have," Rochelle said.

Tir nodded.

"I'm going to see if I can use it." Marlys raised the platter and cast a locator spell. She saw Kelsie within the platter's shiny surface. She sat on a bench next to Voni.

"I don't understand why we don't just attack Argent," Kelsie said. "We know where he is. We have weapons."

"We need to attack wisely, Kelsie," Voni said, "to protect ourselves and innocents. Marlys, Thorne, Serena, and Rochelle are far better at these sorts of plans. When they know the time is right, they'll take action."

"I want to help," Kelsie said.

"You will," Voni asked. "Marlys wouldn't have come here to test you with the hook if she didn't intend to include you in her plans. Be patient."

Kelsie pouted.

The image faded.

Marlys returned the platter to the bag.

Rochelle turned to Serena. "What about the prism?"

"I didn't want to get everyone wet trying it out," Serena said.

Thorne snorted. "We're sorcerers. We can keep ourselves dry."

"There's always the possibility that the artifact can defeat such a spell," Serena said.

"I'll take the chance," Thorne said. "I'd like to see what it does."

The sorcerers voiced their agreement.

"Very well." Serena took out the prism.

"We can wring moisture from the air with sorcery," Tir said, "as long as the air itself is not dry. How is this different?"

"The book says the artifact will seek water from whatever distance it needs to." Serena looked up. "But we have clouds above us. Not rain clouds, but clouds, nonetheless. The device will not have to go far."

Marlys cast a spell to repel water. The other sorcerers did likewise.

"The amount of rain, the spell book says, depends on how much power one pours into the prism," Serena said. "I'll increase the magic I feed into it gradually."

"I have an idea," Zaria said. "I'll go out to the road and see how far the rain spreads." She cast an end point spell and was gone.

Serena held the prism at arm's length and summoned her powers. Marlys scanned her surroundings to see drizzle coming down around her. The clouds remained a brilliant white and the sky between them remained blue. However, the clouds seemed to have shrunk slightly.

As Serena intensified the magic directed to the prism, the drizzle slowly intensified to a steady rain. With more power focused on the prism, the rain became a downpour.

Serena drew the prism back as she stopped channeling her magical power into it. The rain stopped.

Marlys looked up. The clouds had diminished to wisps. She canceled the water-repelling spell.

Rochelle pointed. "The grounds have puddles. The grass in the clearing is wet, and the leaves on the trees beyond are dripping water."

Zaria stepped out of the end point spell. "No rain where I was. The road is dry, but the path near the fortress is soaked."

"The rain doesn't extend too far, then," Tir said.

Rochelle nodded. "It may be enough to dampen an attack, literally."

Serena put the prism back in the bag. "That's the reason we brought it back."

The next morning, after breakfast, Celestine gathered the apprentices in the classroom. Other sorcerers tended to animals and gathered fruit and vegetables for future meals. Marlys sat at her desk recording the events of the day before.

Edwina's image appeared to Marlys while she wrote.

"Marlys! Cullen just told me that he discovered a group of three families set off down the road just after sunrise."

"No sorcerers with them, I presume," Marlys said.

"No. They left on their own, heading toward Valleyview. According to their neighbors, they thought if the tradespeople had gone out and back safely, they could too."

Marlys sighed. "Where are they?"

"We cast locator spells. They're on the road near the Northpoint travel shelter."

"Did you send sorcerers there?"

"No. Every sorcerer here wanted to go, but I told them that if Argent was there, he could kill them all before they could cast a single spell and they would end up helping no one. That's the reason I called you."

Marlys nodded. "We'll be there as soon as we can."

"Let me know if we can help."

"Absolutely."

When Edwina's image faded, Marlys sorcerously rang the bell in the fortress, signaling the sorcerers to gather. She hurried out and down the stairs to the audience room.

Serena and Rochelle were already there.

"What is it?" Serena asked.

"Citizens on the road, unaccompanied by sorcerers." Marlys moved to the armory and reached for the vambrace and the bludgeon.

Rochelle groaned. "We knew that would happen!"

"Rochelle," Marlys said as she strapped the vambrace on. "Go to Valleyview and bring Kelsie here."

"I'll be back directly." Rochelle conjured a transportation spell and disappeared into it.

By this time, most of the sorcerers and apprentices had entered the room.

"What's going on?" Celestine asked. The apprentices gathered around her and looked on curiously.

"Citizens going out alone," Serena explained as she strapped on the strength belt.

"Is Argent there?" Thorne asked.

"I haven't cast a locator spell yet," Marlys said. "The citizens are near the Northpoint travel shelter."

Thorne cast the spell. "Argent is by himself, about a half league from Northpoint."

"Much too close," Tir said.

"His men may not be far behind," Marlys said.

Rochelle reappeared with Kelsie and Janna.

"Janna, what are you doing here?" Thorne said.

"I can attack Argent directly," Janna said.

"Seemed like a sensible option," Rochelle said.

"Who's going?" Durand said.

"I'm going," Marlys said, "along with Serena, Rochelle, Zaria, Tir, Thorne, Kelsie, and Janna. Nessa, we need a Librarian to stay here."

Nessa nodded solemnly.

Zaria had a crossbow in hand and a quiver of bolts slung over a shoulder. "I presume Kelsie will handle the hook?"

"Yes," Rochelle said, passing it to Kelsie.

Kelsie squealed with glee as she accepted the artifact.

Marlys stepped over to Kelsie and looked her in the eye. "Kelsie, you're to wait until Serena has defined a protective perimeter with the stake, and stay behind it until instructed. Then gather all the civilians with the hook and return them to Riverglen. You know where that is, don't you?"

Kelsie rolled her eyes. "I've been there hundreds of times."

"Good," Marlys said. "When I say, you can step just outside the barrier to use the hook. I'll be watching out for you while you work. When you've moved everyone, get back behind the barrier and stay there."

Kelsie's brow furrowed. "Can't I do anything?"

"You're using the hook," Marlys said. "That's something. If we need you to do anything else, we'll tell you."

"I can attack Argent, too," Kelsie said.

"We haven't forgotten that," Marlys said. "But wait to act until you're told."

"What if everyone else gets overwhelmed," Kelsie said, "and I'm the only one left?"

"I doubt that will happen," Thorne said.

"Of course you can act if the situation is dire," Marlys said, "but the rest of us are there to see it doesn't come to that."

"Kelsie," Tir said, "every other encounter we've had has resolved quickly. Probably by the time you've moved everyone, the danger will be over."

"Hopefully," Thorne said, "we'll find that Argent hasn't discovered the traveling party yet. Then Kelsie can move them and we can all go home."

"May the Bright Beings confirm your words," Celestine said.

Marlys looked around. "Is everyone equipped? Oh, Tir, hand me the mirror."

Tir reached over to the mirror's place on the wall and gave it Marlys. He took the hammer for himself.

Marlys looked around. Everyone who was to go with her had lined up in preparation for traveling through the portal. All wore determined expressions.

"It looks as if we're ready." Marlys cast the transportation spell. "Let's go."

"May the Bright Beings watch over you," Nessa said as Marlys's team stepped through.

Chapter 17

Upon arriving at Northpoint, the first thing Marlys heard were screams. As Serena quickly set up the protective barrier, Marlys looked to the road. She saw a multitude of Argent's men swarming around the Briarhill party brandishing clubs, knives, and swords. The families were frozen in place. Children clutched at their parents' clothing. Argent's men surged toward the traveler's carts.

"Argent isn't here yet," Thorne said. "But my locator spell shows he's coming."

"I can stop Argent's men long enough for Kelsie to step out of the barrier and move the Briarhill people," Tir said.

"How...?" Kelsie asked as Tir brought down a bolt of lightning from a sunny sky.

The brilliant flash and resounding boom caused everyone on the road to look up and around. A rough circle of scorched earth was visible nearby.

Marlys pulled Kelsie outside the barrier. "Now, Kelsie!"

To her credit, Kelsie immediately sprang into action, snagging the Briarhill party, including carts and animals. They disappeared.

"Tir," Marlys said, pulling Kelsie back inside the barrier, "open a sorcerous channel to Edwina and confirm they've arrived."

"Will do," Tir said.

Meanwhile, on the road, the sudden disappearance of their quarry seemed to confuse Argent's men even more than the sudden lightning did. They turned in circles, gazing up and down and around with puzzled expressions.

"Why are we standing here?" Kelsie said. "They're out there helpless."

"Our efforts need to be concentrated on Argent now," Marlys said. "We're waiting for him to appear."

Tir leaned in Marlys's direction. "Edwina said the Briarhill party appeared just outside the protective barrier around

Riverglen. They're bringing them in. Some injuries, nothing the sorcerers can't heal."

"Thank you, Tir," Marlys said.

Meanwhile, Argent's men spotted the sorcerers standing on the hill. The attackers left the road and ran up the incline, shouting and waving their weapons.

"They're coming this way!" Kelsie said.

"Let them," Thorne said. "They can't hurt us."

"At least let's confuse them," Kelsie said. "I can conjure a thrumming spell." She lifted her arms.

"Kelsie, no!" Marlys said.

Too late. Kelsie, inexperienced, seemed to have forgotten about the barrier. The thrumming spell resounded inside the perimeter and did not reach Argent's men. Marlys and the other sorcerers covered their ears, temporarily disoriented by their ringing eardrums. Thorne dropped the mace.

Kelsie, unaffected due to her casting a protective spell around herself, dropped the hook and picked up the mace. She strode outside the barrier and ran toward the men. As she sprinted in their direction, she aimed the mace and made hammering motions. One after another, men dropped to the ground.

"Kelsie, come back!" Janna shouted.

Kelsie either did not hear or ignored the warning. Her expression was exuberant as men fell on either side of her.

Marlys slowly recovered her wits from the thrumming spell. She rummaged on the ground for the hook. Picking it up, she stepped just outside the barrier.

"Argent!" Thorne called.

He stood alone on the road, battle axe in one hand, shield over the other arm. He surveyed the scene with a scowl and looked around, apparently to spot who had caused his men to collapse.

Serena disappeared into a transportation spell.

Zaria had a bolt ready and aimed it at Argent.

Marlys moved the hook to snag Kelsie.

Argent aimed the battle axe at Kelsie and made a chopping motion. Behind him, Serena appeared, wrenched the battle axe from Argent's hand, and disappeared again. Argent moved backwards slightly when Serena took the battle axe, causing the crossbow bolt to miss and fly off toward the woods.

Marlys pulled Kelsie to the barrier. Rochelle and Tir grabbed Kelsie's sagging body and carried her inside it, lowering her to the ground. Marlys aimed the hook at Argent. Zaria aimed the crossbow again. Argent pulled out his own hook. In one motion, Argent used the hook to encircle himself and his men. The instant before Marlys could snag Argent, they all disappeared. Zaria's crossbow bolt passed through the space Argent had just vacated.

Hurrying back inside the barrier, Marlys knelt next to Kelsie. Janna already sat at Kelsie's head, sobbing uncontrollably. Thorne stood behind Janna, looking down. Marlys put a hand on Kelsie's chest but could detect no sign of life.

"She can't be dead," Marlys whispered. "I pulled her back."

"I'm sorry, Marlys," Thorne said. "Argent acted first."

Serena appeared, carrying the battle axe. She stepped inside the protective barrier.

"Sorry, Serena," Zaria said. "I did my best."

"Your aim was true," Serena said. "I'm sorry that my taking the battle axe moved him out of the path of your bolt."

"We have the battle axe," Rochelle said grimly. "We will lose no one else today."

Serena turned to Kelsie. "Is she...?"

Tir nodded.

They all bowed their heads and folded their hands in front of them in a few moments of silence. Janna's sobs diminished.

"We have to take her back to Valleyview," Thorne said.

"I'll break the news at the fortress and contact the other regions," Serena said. "I need to go back there now and secure the battle axe so that it can't be used again."

Rochelle bent down. "Marlys?"

Marlys heard and saw everything, but found she could not move or speak.

"Go," Tir said to Serena. "We'll manage everything here."

Serena disappeared into a transportation spell.

Thorne stepped over to Marlys and pulled her up. "Valleyview," was all she said.

Thorne cast a spell for extra strength, bent down, and lifted Kelsie.

Tir cast the transportation spell. Thorne led the way. Rochelle helped Janna up and held her as they followed Thorne. Zaria put an arm around Marlys and guided her toward the portal. Tir followed them.

They all appeared just outside the training center. Janna let them in through the barrier and opened the front door. Thorne walked in and laid Kelsie gently on a padded bench.

Marlys heard gasps of horror and exclamations of "What happened?" "Is Kelsie all right?" "Oh, no!"

Silently, Marlys grasped a chair and sat near Kelsie's head. She cast a preserving spell. Taking Kelsie's dead hand, she found it was still warm.

Looking at Kelsie's face, Marlys went over the events leading to her death. Could she have done anything more? She was not overly fond of Kelsie, true, but she had not wanted Kelsie dead, either. In fact, she had started to warm towards Kelsie. Kelsie had such promise as a sorcerer. Now that potential had been extinguished.

Marlys sat beside Kelsie for an undetermined amount of time. Someone pressed a mug of tea into her free hand. She grasped the cup, but did not look up to see who had given it to her or speak words of thanks. She sipped at the tea, warm, as Kelsie's hand grew cold.

Kelsie had been her responsibility. She had failed. It was a bitter thought.

Marlys began to perceive conversation around her for the first time since she had arrived. She turned toward Thorne, who was speaking to Janna.

"Janna, we all are grieved at the loss of Kelsie. We all knew that Kelsie took risks, heedless of any advice. Her fate was a result of being so headstrong, and should surprise no one."

Thorne might have felt that her words would comfort Janna. Instead, Janna began to wail again.

Marlys released Kelsie's hand and set the mug on an armrest. She silently stood, walked over to Janna, and embraced her tightly. They wept on each other's shoulders.

When Marlys and Janna had regained their composure, Marlys led Janna to a couch. They sat next to each other.

Janna spoke first. Without looking at Marlys, Janna said, "When you first came here, I thought you were soft. You needed hardening. Kelsie and I did what we could, but you went your own way."

Marlys remained silent. What could she say to that?

Janna continued, "When you released us from the time bind, I was afraid. I thought you would seek revenge on me, on Kelsie, on Thorne. But you didn't. You were kind to us." Janna turned her head toward Marlys. "I found you had become strong in your own way. Elspeth and Voni told us there was another path to sorcery. I learned that from the other apprentices and the sorcerers you had trained. I still think you're too soft in places. I still think I was right in trying to harden you. But I cannot deny that you and Serena over there..." she waved in Serena's direction, "...are the mightiest sorcerers south of the Library."

Marlys knew that this was as close to an apology as she would ever get from Janna. "Whatever else passed between us, I value you as a sorcerer." She nodded in Kelsie's direction. "I valued Kelsie as well. I am heartily sorry I will never have the chance to see what she would have become. I look forward to seeing what sort of sorcerer you will become."

Janna nodded. She stood and smoothed her clothes. "I will pay my respects to Kelsie now." She walked away.

Marlys stood.

Thorne joined her. "I see now that I owe you an apology."

Marlys raised an eyebrow. Was Thorne about to confess how cruelly she had treated her?

"I said after we lost Elspeth that you hated her," Thorne said. "That was rash." She paused, then forced out her next words. "That was untrue." She paused again. "And I am sorry."

"Thank you." Marlys nodded. *And that,* Marlys thought, *is as close to an apology as I'll ever get from Thorne.*

It was enough.

Thorne reached out and put a hand on Marlys's upper arm. "Kelsie's death is not your fault. You did everything you could to protect her. We did everything we could to protect her. She was the one who took the risk. Sometimes you cannot save someone from themselves."

Marlys did not answer. Her mind recognized the validity of what Thorne had said, but her heart remained skeptical.

Thorne let go of her arm.

Serena came over and handed Marlys a mug of tea. "The battle axe is secure at the fortress. I laid it in an empty wooden box and placed it in a room at the lowest underground level. Then I secured it with the strongest spells I knew."

"I agree it needs to be secured," Thorne said, "but I would prefer that it be more easily accessible so that we can use it against Argent."

"We can't use it against him as long as he has that shield," Serena said. "Besides, it's too dangerous to have around. It would be too easy for someone to accidentally point it at someone else. I myself handled it delicately and told everyone at the fortress to get away from me until it was stored. No, it belongs in the vault at the Library where it cannot be reached except in extreme need."

Genevieve stood in Marlys's line of sight. Upon hearing Serena mention the Library, she turned and joined them. "I agree. Bring it to the Library and we'll open the vault. While you are there, you are welcome to read the forbidden spell books."

Thorne's head drew back in surprise. "I didn't expect you to open it to us so easily."

"Not 'us,'" Genevieve said. "Serena. And this is not something we've easily given permission for. We have lost two sorcerers. We are under siege. The people of this continent have been held hostage, looted, intimidated. This cannot go on. Our efforts so far have failed to resolve the situation. We must explore any option available to us."

"Thank you," Marlys said.

"Once we have observed the proprieties with Kelsie," Serena said, "I'll take the battle axe to the Library vault and read the spell books there."

"Be sure you are prepared to read them," Genevieve said, "those who have read them in the distant past left writings behind that they regretted doing so. There is much sorrow and horror within, and once read, the words will not be easily forgotten."

"I'm determined to do whatever needs to done to defeat Argent," Serena said. "I'll have little regret when he is gone, but great regret if I could have sped his overthrow and failed to do so."

"Would that I could go there and read the books," Thorne said. "I would have no regrets whatsoever."

Genevieve looked Thorne in the eye. "That is a reason among many that you aren't reading them."

Thorne sighed and walked away.

Genevieve shook her head and turned to rejoin the other Librarians milling around.

Marlys lifted her head. The Valleyview center was as crowded now as it was when they mourned Elspeth. She particularly noticed another knot of High Sorcerers talking together.

Tir moved within her range of sight, drawing Marlys's attention. "I went back and found the mace lying on the ground. I returned it to the fortress."

"We think that it remained where Kelsie dropped it when Argent took her life," Rochelle said. "All of Argent's men who were anywhere near it were flat on the ground when Argent whisked them away. They won't be bothering us for some time. We'll have peace for at least a few days."

"I wonder if Argent has enough regard for his men to heal them," Tir said.

Serena said, "Argent made a considerable effort to bring them here. I doubt he would let them die."

Ilse approached them. "Marlys, we've had a conference of the High Sorcerers. No disrespect intended, but you seemed to be in deep mourning and we wished to respect that."

"No disrespect taken. Thank you," Marlys said.

"To go directly to the point," Ilse said, "we want Argent gone. Now. We are willing to do anything to bring that about. We also know Argent is well protected. We agree that those of you in Goldenvalley are best suited to defeat him. All of us have exchanged ideas and discussed strategies for weeks, but none of them seem likely to work. We will do anything that you deem necessary, even if it means gathering every sorcerer on the continent as an army to surround him."

Genevieve approached. "I wish that could assure the victory. However, our records of the sorcerous wars tell us such a confrontation would not necessarily be successful."

Serena faced Ilse. "Marlys and I have retrieved more sorcerous weapons from the island worlds, weapons Argent has no ability to wield. Once we have laid Sorcerer Kelsie to rest, I will go to the Library and read their forbidden spell books. Tradition holds that they reveal how the sorcerous wars were won."

Ilse lifted an eyebrow. "Legend also says that victory came at the cost of casting loathsome spells. Are you prepared for that?"

"We are," Marlys said, surprising herself when the words came out of her mouth with confidence.

"Good!" Ilse said. "So are we. We wanted to be sure you would not shirk in defeating Argent even if you had a vile spell in hand that would do so."

"We will, however," Marlys said, "consider this possibility thoughtfully and wisely before acting."

"We expect nothing less." Ilse inclined her head in farewell and walked away.

"I shudder to think about it," Tir said, "but the thought had crossed my mind as well. What cost would I be willing to pay to defeat Argent?"

Marlys turned her head toward Kelsie's body, lying stiff and cold on the bench. "I don't think I could live with myself if I had to endure another needless death. No spell would make me feel worse."

Chapter 18

As the daylight outside waned, those who had come to honor Kelsie began to leave for home. Sorcerers and apprentices from all over the continent had come to pay their respects. By dusk, only those from Valleyview and the Goldenvalley fortress remained.

Marlys approached Voni. "Will you be all right here without us?"

Voni nodded. "I think everyone at Valleyview would prefer to be left on our own tonight. We'll have everything prepared for the funeral tomorrow."

"We'll return then." Marlys gave Voni a hug. She gestured to those from the fortress to follow before opening the transportation spell.

When they arrived at the fortress, Marlys felt surprised to see Thorne had come through behind her.

"Not remaining at Valleyview?" Marlys said. "I think you could if you wished."

Thorne shook her head. "I seem to have made myself an annoyance by my words about Kelsie."

Marlys opened her mouth to reply, but found herself at a loss for words.

Thorne shrugged and waved a hand. "It would not be the first time," she said resignedly.

"Will you go to the memorial?" Marlys asked.

"Yes, but I'll limit my activity to my presence. They all know that I had warm feelings toward Kelsie. They just don't want to be reminded at this time that I also held her accountable. Janna will act as lead mourner."

The next morning, everyone at the fortress assembled and stepped through the transportation spell to Valleyview, arriving just outside the barrier. They joined an assembly of sorcerers and apprentices from all over the continent.

They all turned toward the training center door as it opened. Four sorcerers carried a litter holding Kelsie's wrapped body. Voni created an opening in the barrier and the guests flowed inside, filling the area between the barrier and the building. They silently followed the litter.

The sorcerers reached the grave and set the litter on the ground next to it. Marlys stepped forward and canceled the preservation spell. The sorcerers used ropes to lower the body into the hole.

When they all drew back, Janna stepped forward and raised her arms. "We honor you, Kelsie." After the guests repeated the words, she continued, "You will remain in our memory." Again, the onlookers echoed the phrase. "We release you to the glorious realm of the Bright Beings."

Voni came forward and handed an evergreen tree sapling to Janna. Janna held it in place as the sorcerers filled the grave with earth. Once the tree had been planted, all stepped back and observed a moment of silence before the singers among the sorcerers came forward to vocalize the traditional farewell.

Marlys noted that the Valleyview assembly had placed Kelsie's grave next to Elspeth's, which she thought was fitting.

Voni faced the guests. "Thank you, all, for honoring our sister. You are welcome to share a meal with us in her memory." She led the way indoors.

Janna sat at the head of the table as the meal commenced. In contrast to Elspeth, who had been known by many throughout the continent, especially the older sorcerers, few had known Kelsie well. Nonetheless, some of the Valleyview sorcerers and apprentices shared memories of Kelsie. They spoke of her playful nature and willingness to learn. Marlys could not help but think that "playful" had been a euphemism for "mischievous." On the other hand, Voni and Elspeth had confided to Marlys privately that Kelsie had moderated her behavior once she had been surrounded by new companions, and never returned to the nasty pranks that Marlys had known her to pull.

Edwina stood to address Janna. "Kelsie rescued the party from Briarhill with her proficiency in using the hook artifact. The families she saved, as well as the sorcerers and apprentices in Briarhill, including me, wish me to express their heartfelt gratitude and condolences."

Janna smiled slightly and nodded.

Marlys rose. "For my part, I felt that Kelsie had great potential and I am sincerely sorry that she was taken from us before she could reach her greatest skill in sorcery."

Janna, as lead mourner, had the last word. "Kelsie was my best and truest friend. At times, she was my only friend. Without her company and encouragement, I would not have become the sorcerer I am today. May the Bright Beings welcome her into their arms."

When the memorial meal was complete, Janna rose from her chair. The guests stood and formed a line at the door. Janna stood at the exit with Voni, receiving farewells and warm expressions of sympathy as their guests walked out.

Marlys took a place at the end of the line. She took both of Janna's hands in hers as she expressed her condolences again to Voni and Janna.

Janna returned Marlys's grip tightly and looked Marlys in the eye. "Now let's go get that murderer."

Marlys gave Janna's hand one last squeeze. "I promise you, we will." She walked out into the yard where Frieda was minding the barrier opening. After exchanging a nod with Frieda, Marlys joined the Goldenvalley fortress residents who were waiting for her and cast a transportation spell.

At the fortress, Marlys and the others emerged from the transportation spell and walked to the audience room. There, they separated. Some went to their rooms, others headed toward the kitchen for tea and cakes.

Tir joined Marlys as she headed toward the kitchen. "By the way, last night I cast a locator spell for Argent and looked into the platter."

Marlys lifted an eyebrow. "Oh? What did you see?"

"Enough to gather that the party from Briarhill accidentally ran into Argent's men. Argent had ordered them to scout around the area, to look for an old abandoned fortress Argent heard about in his childhood. Argent himself went ahead to find a place where they could harvest stone or make bricks to repair it."

"He must have been trying to find the ruins south of Northpoint," Marlys said as she took a cup of tea from Rochelle. "I myself have occasionally thought of rebuilding there."

"That's all the information I gleaned before the image on the platter faded." Tir accepted the cup Rochelle held out to him.

Rochelle sipped from her own cup. "What of the men Kelsie felled with the mace?"

"I only had a brief glimpse," Tir said. "I saw men lying on the stone floor of the underground chamber. Argent grumbled at having to revive so many."

"Thank you for telling me," Marlys said.

Serena approached Marlys. "If you're willing, I want to go to the Library of Sorcery with the battle axe now."

Marlys halted and faced Serena. "This soon?"

"Yes, with your permission," Serena said. "My determination to read the books is strong right now and I want to go before the feeling passes."

Celestine had been lingering over her tea near Rochelle as Tir had given his account. She took a sip of tea from her mug and faced Serena. "You may have more focused attention if you let your umbrage cool a little."

Serena shook her head. "I don't think I could eat or sleep or do anything else until I've at least started to read those books."

Marlys considered a moment before nodding. "If that's the case, I can go with you now. Celestine, you're in charge while we're gone."

Celestine nodded. "How long do you intend to stay?"

"I'll stay long enough to open the vault and secure the battle axe," Marlys said. "Then I'll return."

"Reading spell books is not a group endeavor, in any case," Serena said. "For these books, I'd prefer reading alone and undisturbed."

"Do you want to pack a bag first?" Marlys asked.

"I've had one packed ever since we lost Elspeth," Serena said. "I just have to grab it."

"Shall we retrieve the battle axe, then?" Marlys said.

"Yes. I could move it by myself, but it is awkward."

"If you don't mind," Rochelle said, "I'll get your bag from your room while you and Marlys get the battle axe. I'll meet you in the audience hall."

"That would help," Serena said. "Thank you."

Serena led Marlys to a room on the lower level of the fortress. By sorcerous light, Marlys saw a long wooden box on the floor.

There were handholds on all four sides. Serena grasped a handle on the longer side. Marlys took one on the opposite side. They made their way to the audience room where Rochelle waited holding Serena's travel bag.

Rochelle handed Serena the bag and hugged her. "May the Bright Beings give you courage and wisdom for your task."

"Thank you," Serena said as Rochelle took a step back.

Marlys opened a sorcerous channel. "Genevieve, Serena and I are coming now."

"We're ready for you," Genevieve said.

Marlys and Serena again took up the wooden box. Marlys cast the transportation spell.

Marlys and Serena arrived on the Library grounds. Genevieve and Blair stood waiting for them.

"Here, let me take your bag," Blair said.

Serena handed it to him. "Thank you."

Carrying the box, Marlys and Serena followed Genevieve and Blair to the vault. Blair put Serena's bag on the cave floor. He and Genevieve cast the spells to nullify the barriers around the vault. Genevieve retrieved the key from her pocket, unlocked the door, and pulled it open.

Marlys and Serena walked in with the box. The sorcerous light was dim. Blair cast a lighting spell so they could see better.

They all surveyed the room.

"No one has been inside this vault for generations," Genevieve said. "We've only opened the door and peered inside on occasion."

To her left, Marlys saw a stack of wooden boxes of various sizes. She inclined her head in that direction. "Let's put the box there."

"Those must be where forbidden weapons are stored." Serena said.

They set the box down next to the stack. Looking around, Marlys saw a multitude of shelves on the walls, all holding books.

"Shelves upon shelves of books," Blair remarked.

"There's a wide desk with a comfortable-looking chair," Marlys observed.

"And all dust-free," Genevieve said. "The preservation spell must have been a strong one."

Blair handed Serena her bag. "Do you have what you need?"

Serena set the bag on the floor. "Let me check one more thing." She found a drawer on the desk. She pulled it out. "Writing paper, ink, pen." She turned and looked at the others. "Yes, I have what I need."

"I'll set a sentry spell so that no one can come near without your being alerted," Blair said.

"We prepared the same room in the Library residence that you had the last time you were here," Genevieve said. "Feel free to seal the vault, come back to the Library, and sleep in the evenings."

"If you need a meal, water, tea, anything while you're here, just open a sorcerous channel to us," Blair said.

"Thank you," Serena said.

Marlys hugged Serena. When she let go, she said, "May the Bright Beings watch over you, Serena."

"May they watch over all of us," Serena said.

"We'll leave you to your work," Genevieve said.

Marlys followed Genevieve and Blair out. They left the door open so that Serena would have air. Blair cast the sentry spell.

"I'll return to the fortress," Marlys said. "If you need me, open a channel."

Genevieve nodded. "I shall. May the Bright Beings watch over us all."

After Marlys returned to the fortress, the day passed peacefully. Some sorcerers lingered in the kitchen and dining hall. Others felt the need for more weapons practice. Marlys joined those sorcerers and the apprentices who wished to observe.

Marlys heard nothing from Serena for the rest of the day. Lyra and Astrid reported no movement from Argent, which Tir confirmed through the platter.

The next morning, Marlys took a turn at kitchen duty. She helped to prepare and serve the food. She sat with the others to eat. When the meal was over, she took part in clearing the tables and cleaning up. She had placed the last of the washed cups from the midday meal on the shelf when she heard a chime. She looked up and around.

Nessa, who also shared kitchen duty that day, said, "That must be the sentinel stone."

"Let's look outside," Marlys said.

"While you're checking the front," Nessa said. "I'll run to the roof and see if there's anyone else in the distance."

Marlys nodded. She hurried toward the entryway of the fortress to look out a window. She saw a lone man walking on the road. He carried no pack, had no animals with him. His wore black pants, a beige button-down shirt, a green felt hat with a feather, and ankle-height brown boots.

Sensing movement close behind her, she turned to see Durand and Tir peering over her shoulder.

Durand gestured. "He's turning up the walk."

"I suppose I need to go out and meet him," Marlys said.

"Wear the chest protector," Tir advised.

"Good idea." Marlys walked to the armory and put it on.

"I have the stone from Overlook which tells if someone's inner mood and outer demeanor match." Durand extended it to her.

Marlys took it. "I'll also cast a truth spell."

Nessa ran down the stairs toward them, breathing hard. "There's no one else as far as the eye can see."

"That can be misleading," Tir said. "Anyone could be hiding in the wooded areas nearby."

Nessa nodded. "But at least we know this much."

"Thank you, Nessa," Marlys said.

Rochelle approached. "Going to see who our visitor is?"

"Yes," Marlys said.

"I'll be right behind you," Rochelle said.

"I'm not going outside the barrier unless necessary," Marlys said. "We can talk through it."

"Nonetheless, I'll feel easier if I'm with you." Rochelle said.

"Very well," Marlys said.

When Marlys opened the front door, she saw the man pounding against the invisible barrier, which had blocked his progress.

"Venerable sorcerers! I must speak with you!"

"I'm coming," Marlys said as she walked down the stairs to the barrier. As she drew closer, she recognized the man as Grady, the one Argent had spoken with when they monitored him with the lance. She stopped on the other side of the barrier, holding the stone. Looking into it, she saw Grady's image. The face of the image wore an agitated expression.

"What is it that you need to speak with us about?" Marlys asked.

Grady took his hat out, held it over his chest, and bowed. "Venerable sorcerer."

"What is it that you want?" Marlys repeated.

He looked around nervously. "Inside, please?"

"Are you being watched?" Marlys asked.

"Not that I know of, but I must be cautious."

"Stretch out your arms," Rochelle said.

Hat still in one hand, Grady did so.

Marlys opened the barrier and stepped out with Rochelle. As Marlys cast a truth spell, Rochelle patted the man's sides and legs.

"I am unarmed," Grady said timidly.

Rochelle nodded. "Put your arms down."

Grady did so. With his eyes focused on Marlys, he put his hat back on.

"I'm Marlys, the High Sorcerer of this region." She gestured to Rochelle. "This is Rochelle, another sorcerer here."

Grady bowed again. "I am Grady."

Marlys refrained from telling him she already knew his name. This revelation might make him more nervous than he was already. She waved at him. "Follow me." She turned and headed back into the fortress. Grady walked a step behind and to one side. Rochelle strode behind him. Nessa joined them at the doorway.

When Grady stepped into the hall, he was instantly in awe. His mouth fell open slightly as his gaze went from the carpets, the light cast through the stained glass windows, and the ornate, vaulted ceiling. His posture stiffened slightly as he curiously eyed Tir and Durand as they stepped in this direction. Grady regarded the two other men with curiosity and courtesy.

Marlys led Grady to the dining hall, now empty, and motioned for him to sit. At the same time, she heard a growling sound from his stomach.

"Are you hungry?" she asked.

"It's nothing," Grady said.

Consulting the stone, Marlys was given the impression that Grady was indeed hungry. She nodded to a seat. "Sit and we'll bring you something."

"I'll get it." Tir walked to the kitchen.

Other sorcerers and apprentices gathered around the table, including Thorne. Grady eyed them nervously.

Marlys turned to them. "I think our guest would prefer a smaller audience. Rochelle, Durand, Nessa, Thorne, and Tir can stay. I'll inform you about our conversation later."

The others walked out to the classrooms or the audience room. Those doors, however, remained open and Marlys knew they would be able to hear from the other rooms.

Grady let out a breath and seemed more relaxed.

Marlys sat next to Grady, over an arm's length away. She set the stone on the table in front of her. "I presume you can eat our food."

Grady's brow furrowed. "Why not?"

"The world you come from is a different world," Marlys said.

He drew in his chin. "Not different. The same."

Chapter 19

Marlys's brow furrowed. "The same world? Yours and ours?"

Grady looked confused. "Every school child knows that the Bright Beings separated our worlds in the faraway times. Two worlds, from one."

"We didn't know that," Marlys said. "Can you tell us?"

"I can do that, venerable sorcerer," Grady said. "But with humility, and with respect, I wish to beg a favor of you. That is why I came."

Tir returned. He set a plate of food and a mug of cider in front of Grady. Grady surveyed the plate hungrily, looked at Marlys, and turned back to the meal in front of him.

Marlys motioned to the plate. "We can talk while you eat."

Grady picked up a bread roll and broke it. "As you wish, venerable sorcerer."

Marlys felt unaccustomed to such deference, but she felt it was to her advantage to allow it. "Two worlds, from one, you said. Tell us how that came about."

"The Bright Beings value peace and tranquility," Grady began.

"Yes, they do," Marlys said.

"In the beginning, they created sorcery and gifted certain mortals with magical powers, greater and lesser," Grady said.

"As it is here," Marlys said.

"To promote harmony, they also set a spell that allows us to understand each other, and read each other's writings," Grady said.

"It is the same here," Marlys said.

"At first, all was well. Sorcerers helped commoners. Commoners provisioned sorcerers. After a time, sorcerers began to quarrel."

"Over what?" Durand asked.

"How the world would be run. Senior sorcerers, brother and sister, Boyd and Beryl, clashed. Other sorcerers and commoners took one side or the other. Quarrels became hostile. Boyd's sorcerers raised armies. Some proclaimed themselves rulers over a territory. They enforced their power harshly. They battled each other to expand their territories. The Bright Beings were greatly offended. They separated the worlds. Each world was given a center of sorcery where the sorcerers would be stronger and would be tasked with keeping the peace and preventing wars in their own way."

"What was the quarrel about?" Marlys said, realizing that Grady had not fully answered Durand's question.

"Boyd believed that the world would run best if sorcerers ruled. Sorcerers at a central location would rule over all. Sorcerers accountable to the central sorcerers would rule in local regions. Their word would be law. Their decisions would be final. Lawbreakers would be punished according to the severity of the crime. In that way, Boyd said, order would be established. Peace would be maintained."

"Sounds like a good system to me," Thorne said.

"We live well, for the most part," Grady said. "The sorcerers at the capital act strongly if widespread violence threatens to erupt. The roads are safe. There are rogues, yes. Mortals are imperfect. The Bright Beings know that. But there are not many ruffians and they can only get away with so much. Arguments are confined within local communities. Local communities can act as they wish as long as they obey the rules of the capital."

"The men who attacked us initially seemed belligerent enough," Rochelle said. "Your ruffians may be relatively few, but they are capable of inflicting injury."

Grady looked apologetic. "That was not me. That was not most of us. It is true that Argent sought out rogues on my world to aid him and brought them with him. Most of us, though, are farmers and herders and artisans. We're husbands and fathers. We serve Argent only because he forced us to."

"Doesn't sound as if this worked well for you, with Argent," Rochelle said.

"When he first arrived, Argent helped us, and he still does. He made it easier to harvest. He cleared stopped wells, repaired bridges. Healed diseases and injuries. Only recently has he made troublesome demands in exchange."

"And the sorcerers at the capital do nothing?" Thorne asked.

"They came and warned him that he could act as he wished locally, but would not be allowed to spread his aggression outside our community. If there were casualties among us, he would be dealt with severely. The ruffians he enlisted to help him are not allowed to harm us."

"I see. They're allowed only to harm everyone here," Rochelle said.

Grady looked abashed.

"The system has its weaknesses," Thorne said, "but I must say I think the method of enforcement is effective."

Rochelle turned to Thorne. "It seems they allow Argent to compel forced labor, though only locally."

Marlys turned to Grady. "Now tell us about Beryl. What did she want?"

"Beryl wanted two systems. Sorcerers would make rules for sorcerers and discipline their own. Commoners would make rules for commoners and deal with their own. Sorcerers would help commoners with sorcery. Commoners would help sorcerers with provisions. Cooperation would reign. Mutual respect and understanding would result in both sides being satisfied."

"I prefer that way," Durand said.

"The result was that Boyd and his faction were sent to your world and Beryl and her faction stayed in this one, I presume?" Marlys said.

Grady nodded and bit into a chicken leg. He chewed and swallowed. "Sorcerers desiring consensus remained in this world. Sorcerers desiring supremacy were moved to my world."

"Yes, but how does that explain the sorcerous wars here?" Rochelle asked.

Grady finished his bread roll. "The separation was presumed to be incomplete. At first, sorcerers in our world thought that no commerce was possible between our world and yours. For a long time, it was so. Then sorcerers began coming to us from your world. In ones, in twos. Not many, and rarely, but they came. Our sorcerers tried to see if there was a way to travel from my world to yours, but failed. The sorcerers coming to our world also believed in strong rule. At the capital, the sorcerers proudly said that movement was only allowed in our direction because ours was the better way."

"Then, your sorcerers deemed the separation incomplete because sorcerers remained on our world who desired supremacy?" Marlys asked.

Grady paused to take a sip of cider. "Yes. Centuries ago, a large group of sorcerers appeared on our world from yours. They told a tale of conflict. The sorcerers at the capital presumed that not all of Boyd's faction had come to my world when the worlds separated. Those left on your world passed down Boyd's way to their successors through the ages. These were the sorcerers who came to our world after the wars here. The sorcerers on my world instructed the sorcerers from your world in our ways. They accepted our world's conditions. After that, again, our world only saw sorcerers from yours in ones and twos and only rarely."

"I think I can fill in the gap," Nessa said.

Everyone turned to her.

"From my readings of the sorcerous wars in the legends and histories I read at the Library," Nessa said, "I can tell where the narratives merge. We all know that in the very distant past, occasionally someone would try to raise an army, but the resistance was so great the effort came to nothing. These must have been the sorcerers who preferred Boyd's way, but never had enough of a following to impose their will. Until the sorcerous wars, that is, when apparently sorcerers following Boyd's way found the means to strike."

"We've had peace since," Marlys said, "at least, until Argent."

"Everyone has worked hard over the centuries to maintain that peace," Durand said.

Grady looked at Marlys. "There is another difference in our worlds."

Marlys turned to him. "What would that be?"

"Most of the sorcerers on my world are men."

"No women sorcerers?" Marlys asked.

Grady shrugged. "I had heard of women sorcerers, but only have seen them here. You seem to have a great many, meaning no disrespect, venerable sorcerer."

"No disrespect taken," Marlys said.

"Ah," Nessa said. "This also explains the histories I read. The accounts say little about gender, but when they mention the gender of the attackers, there are men included."

Durand turned to Nessa. "Were there men on the defending side?"

Nessa nodded. "Oh, yes. In fact, most of the weapons we have here," she gestured to the armory, "were fashioned by men."

"The accounts I read along the Spell Passage indicated that male sorcerers were more common in the distant past," Tir said. "It would make sense there were men on both sides."

Grady drained what was left of the cider and wiped his mouth with a napkin. He turned to Marlys. "Thank you for the meal. If I have now answered your questions, venerable sorcerer, I wish to present my request to you."

"By all means, tell us," Marlys said.

"Please have mercy on us," Grady said. "I know that you must harbor great anger because of the death of two sorcerers, but I promise that was Argent's will, not ours."

"The ruffians with you have looted and threatened us and our citizens," Rochelle pointed out. "It is not only Argent."

Grady bowed his head briefly. "I have great regret about all of that. I say again, most of us serve Argent only because he forced us to. Please do not kill us. Many are still recovering from being felled by your sorcerer. We have had to plead with Argent to heal and revive them. We are guilty only of trusting Argent when he came to our world and helped us with harvests and other sorcerous favors. We had no idea he would compel us to aid him in harming others to repay him."

"Does Argent know you're here?" Rochelle said.

Grady shook his head. "He sent me out as a scout using the sorcerous hook. He wanted me to see if I could find any stray animals to add to our herd."

"Then he'll want to bring you back," Rochelle said.

"He told me he would bring me back at sundown," Grady said. "He may be late. He's not reliable. He's easily distracted."

Marlys had kept an eye on the mood stone. It showed that Grady was sincere. The truth spell also confirmed he was not lying.

"Our goal is to be rid of Argent," Marlys said. "We have no ill will toward anyone who does not attack us."

"It seems, though," Throne said, "that a large number of you have been threatening and attacking us. In our most recent encounter, a large number of men surged toward us, including the husbands and fathers, by your account."

Grady bowed his head and lowered his eyes.

Marlys remained silent, waiting for an answer.

"He threatens us if we do not do his bidding," Grady said softly. "That is why we joined the rogues in the advance."

"Threatens you?" Durand asked. "I thought you said he was forbidden to harm you."

"Threatens not to help us," Grady said.

"I see," Durand said.

Rochelle and Thorne turned to Marlys.

Marlys took a long breath and let it out. According to the spell and the stone, Grady's words remained accurate. "I cannot make any promises. In the heat of conflict, anything can happen. Accidents happen. I can say again, however, that our quarrel is with Argent and our efforts are focused on him. We have no reason to attack any of you or others following Argent, but we will defend ourselves if we are attacked."

Grady nodded. "I understand."

"Is there anything else?" Marlys asked. When Grady did not respond, she added, "If not, you may go."

Grady stood and bowed. "Thank you, venerable sorcerer."

"Wait!" Thorne turned to Marlys. "He can help us."

"He has already risked much by coming to us," Marlys said. "I'm not going to ask him to spy for us, or to try to secretly sabotage Argent, if that's what you're implying."

Grady looked from Thorne to Marlys nervously.

"He has no chance against a sorcerer," Rochelle said. "Let him be."

Thorne sighed.

Marlys turned to Grady. "You may go. Tir, Durand, escort him out."

Grady again took off his hat and bowed low. "Thank you, venerable sorcerers." When Tir and Durand motioned to him, he followed them out.

When they had gone, Thorne said, "He could have been an asset to us."

"He may still be of help to us," Marlys said. "We've assured him we'll do everything we can to keep him and his friends from harm, and he seems to be the sort of person who would not forget a debt."

"Besides," Rochelle said, "we already have the means to spy on Argent."

"In a limited way," Thorne said.

"As a civilian, he's already limited in how he could help us," Marlys said. "Better to let him go."

As Marlys and Thorne talked, other sorcerers and apprentices walked into the dining hall from the audience hall and the classroom.

"Beryl and Boyd? I have heard nothing of them before," Celestine said.

"I haven't read anything about them at the Library so far," Nessa said.

"Perhaps it's just a story," Thorne said.

"Grady sincerely believed it to be true," Marlys said, "though that doesn't mean that whoever passed the story to him wasn't just reciting a twice-told tale."

"What now?" Celestine asked.

"According to Grady, Argent is still healing the men that Kelsie felled," Marlys said. "I'm waiting for Serena to finish reading the spell books at the Library."

"Have you heard anything from her?" Celestine asked.

"Not since I left her there," Marlys said. "I didn't want to interrupt. In the meantime, we continue with our usual tasks."

The next morning, Marlys finished cleaning up the breakfast dishes with the rest of those assigned to kitchen duty that day. On her way back to her room, Genevieve's image appeared before her.

"Marlys, it's Serena. You need to come now."

Chapter 20

Marlys turned to Genevieve's image. "Is Serena injured?"

"Distressed would be a better word," Genevieve said. "She has emerged from the vault. But she has spoken to no one. She takes meals with everyone else, but sits alone, and waves away anyone who tries to join her or speak with her. She goes to her room for sleep and returns to the vault after breakfast. Now she's sitting on a bench in the main library, motionless, staring out into space. She won't answer me or anyone else."

"I'll be there as soon as I can." When Genevieve closed the connection, Marlys walked back to the armory, where Rochelle and Celestine explained the use of the weapons to the apprentices. "I'm going to the Library. Celestine, you're in charge while I'm gone."

Celestine nodded. "When will you return?"

"I don't know," Marlys said. "If I need provisions, the Library will accommodate me."

"Is it about Serena?" Rochelle said.

"Yes," Marlys said. "Genevieve predicted that the contents of the forbidden books would be disturbing. That seems to be the case. I need to speak with Serena."

"If you need help, call," Rochelle said.

Marlys nodded and cast the transportation spell.

"May the Bright Beings guide you," Celestine said.

"Thank you." Marlys stepped into the portal.

Marlys emerged at the Library's entrance.

Genevieve waited there. "Thank you for coming. Serena's been motionless for some time."

"Let me get a tray of tea and some cakes. I'll sit with her and try to determine what's happening."

Genevieve led Marlys to the kitchen.

"Do you have waycakes?" Marlys asked.

"Yes," Genevieve said, "since we learned how to make them, we've kept a supply in the kitchen."

"I'll take a plate of those with the tea."

Once Marlys had the tray ready, Genevieve led her to the main library. They passed several sorcerers and apprentices browsing the shelves. At last, in an alcove, brilliantly lit by sunshine streaming through floor-to-ceiling windows, Marlys saw Serena sitting on a bench. Serena did not acknowledge Marlys's approach, but stared out the windows pensively.

Marlys nodded her thanks to Genevieve.

Genevieve withdrew.

Marlys sat next to Serena. She set the tray on the bench. Picking up a mug of tea, she held it in front of Serena.

At first, Serena remained still. After a few moments, she silently took the mug and sipped.

Marlys took the plate of waycakes from the tray and held that in front of Serena.

Serena grasped a waycake and took a bite.

Marlys took a waycake of her own and sipped from the mug she had brought for herself.

When Serena had finished the cake, she drained the mug and set it on the bench next to her. Leaning back, she sighed.

Marlys waited patiently for Serena to speak.

"Do you remember the flat that we traveled through on the way to the Mountains of Wrath?" Serena said, still unmoving.

"I could never forget it," Marlys said.

"It's a graveyard." Serena turned and faced Marlys.

"A graveyard?"

"At least the part nearest the escarpment." Serena made an up and down motion. "Remember the sheerness of the cliffs?"

"Yes."

"It wasn't always that way. There used to be a stone incline from the valley to the top of the cliffs. A wide road wound up the incline. In the decisive battle of the sorcerous war, the sorcerers of the Library District and their citizen allies arrayed themselves at the cliffs overlooking the valley. The attackers and their citizen allies filled the valley below. The strongest sorcerers among the Librarians came together. Some destroyed the incline. Others opened up the earth below. The attacking sorcerers, their citizen allies, their carts, horses, everything, fell into the pit. The Librarian sorcerers covered the crater with earth."

"Buried alive?" Marlys asked.

Serena tilted her head slightly. "According to the history, one of the Librarian sorcerers made the same exclamation. He was answered with, 'No, we killed them first.'"

"Universe save us," Marlys said.

"Yes," Serena said. "A horrendous act, but it ended the sorcerous wars. I can understand their reasons. While there were a few Librarians on the opposing side, most sorcerers among the attackers were not Librarians. If those attacking sorcerers conquered the Library District, the world would have had a large group of powerful sorcerers without restraint. Their citizen allies would continue to murder, loot, and assault other citizens. Nothing else had deterred them. It was an act of desperation."

"I can imagine," Marlys said.

Serena continued. "The scattered survivors of the attacking side, who had not come to the battle, were easily rounded up and pushed to the island worlds."

"I noted you said 'he' when referring to one of the sorcerers."

Serena nodded. "There were men on either side. Not a large number, but a significant number. Almost all of the citizen allies of the attackers were men."

"In your absence, we had a visit from one of Argent's men, who came secretly to us to beg for mercy. Wait until I give you his account of sorcerers named Beryl and Boyd."

Serena nodded. "I read of them. The Librarian victors placed the account among the forbidden books, thinking that the knowledge about this legend was the spark that ignited the sorcerous wars."

"I can see why later sorcerers reading the forbidden books regretted reading them," Marlys said.

"I regret it," Serena said. "I now know spells that can cause mass destruction."

"One would need the strength," Marlys said. "Genevieve told us that some of the sorcerers at the time of the wars were stronger than you or me."

"That is true," Serena said, "but I also know how to increase sorcerous strength to cast such spells, though there is a cost."

"Genevieve already told us that the sorcerers who made the weapons we used lost the ability to cast spells...permanently," Marlys said. "I take it that that's a consequence."

"It is," Serena said, "and drawing on such strength can also shorten one's lifespan."

Marlys nodded. "I presume there are other spells you would rather not have learned about?"

"Where would I begin?" Serena said. "Spells that could alter a person's mind or temperament."

"I presume those are different from the healing spells we use if someone is hearing voices that aren't there, or can't remember the way home after walking the same route all their lives."

Serena nodded. "When we use those healing spells, the magic finds a flaw in the brain and repairs it. The spells I read about are different even from the calming spells we use for someone in distress. These spells would change someone's very essence."

"Would you mind giving me an example?" Marlys asked. "You don't need to if you don't want to."

Serena took a long breath and let it out slowly. She sat quietly for a few moments before continuing.

"Among the worst of them is to scrub the mind clean," Serena said. "No memory of who they are, what they have done, anything they have learned in their life...gone. Victims would sit all day, having to be led around, taught to eat again, taught to read again, taught to speak again...and there would be limited ability to do even that."

"Terrible indeed."

"Even more terrible is that the spell cannot be reversed," Serena said. "No healing spell will restore what is lost. If one accidentally casts the spell, or regrets casting it later, nothing will bring the victim back."

Marlys sighed and shook her head. She put a hand on Serena's shoulder briefly.

When Marlys put her hand down, Serena continued, "The slightly lesser spells are no less dangerous because they're so tempting. Your neighbor has a temper? Cast a spell so that the neighbor can't get angry. Except there are some things in life that one needs to get angry about. The shopkeeper is too aggressive? Take away the ability to become aggressive. Except if someone tries to cheat or rob the shopkeeper, maybe aggression is needed. Your cousin is selfish? Take that away, too. Except now everyone can take advantage of your cousin. Not a good thing, that."

"I see what you mean," Marlys said.

"Would you pass me another waycake?" Serena said.

Marlys picked up the plate and held toward Serena. "Yes, of course. Reading all that must have been physically and mentally draining."

"I couldn't begin to describe the feelings I experienced," Serena said, taking the cake. "I didn't—don't—feel comfortable telling anyone about it." She faced Marlys. "Except you." She slowly ate the waycake, and held out her empty mug toward Marlys.

Marlys filled the mug from the teapot. "I will keep everything you've told me in confidence." She set the teapot back on the tray.

Serena drank from the mug. "I know. When I finished reading the books, I closed the vault and resealed it. I thought I'd take notes, but I soon realized I couldn't risk anyone finding what I had written."

"Probably just as well that you don't have anything with you to remind you," Marlys said.

Serena took another sip.

"I presume, then, that you found nothing that you would want to use to help defeat Argent," Marlys said.

"To the contrary," Serena said. "There were other spells I read that I would be quite willing to use against him. We can win."

"Good," Marlys put a hand over Serena's. "Can you hold that thought until we get home and discuss it with everyone?"

"Exactly what I had in mind."

Marlys stood and gathered the mugs. "If you can get your things together while I return the tray to the kitchen, we can leave."

Genevieve and other Librarians gathered at the building's entrance to bid farewell to Serena and Marlys. Genevieve reached out to Serena. Serena set down her bag. Genevieve took both of Serena's hands in hers.

"I speak for the sorcerers and apprentices in the Library District when I say that we are grateful to you for reading the forbidden spell books. Marlys tells me that you found something that will help us defeat Argent."

"I did," Serena said in a low voice.

"I wanted to tell you that the Library is also a place of rest for sorcerers," Genevieve continued. "If you ever feel you in need of repose, please don't hesitate to come."

Serena inclined her head in Marlys's direction. "I thank you for your offer, but at the moment, I feel that I have everything I need in Goldenvalley."

"At home. Of course," Genevieve said.

"Don't ever let anyone else into the vault," Serena said firmly, but politely.

Genevieve let go of Serena's hands. "I won't," she reassured her. She picked up her bag. Marlys cast the transportation spell.

When Serena and Marlys stepped out of the portal and walked into the audience room at the Goldenvalley fortress, they were greeted enthusiastically. Many embraced Serena.

After Tir had hugged Serena, he stepped over to Marlys. "We used a locator spell in your absence."

"Argent?"

"No, Grady," Tir said. "Argent moved him back to his underground chambers. Rochelle, Thorne, and I traveled as close to the compound entrance as we felt safe. Grady was right. All kinds of livestock are grazing around the entrance. There's no sense of order. No fencing. No herders."

Thorne spoke up. "Although there could be a spell keeping them from wandering." Thorne looked from Marlys to Serena. "Serena, did you find out anything that can help us?"

"I did," Serena said.

"Serena needs to rest for a while," Marlys said.

"No, I don't," Serena said evenly. "I'm not wasting another moment. Tell me more about Grady."

"Let's all sit first." She nodded toward the door to the dining hall.

Oriana offered to take Serena's bag, which Serena had set on the floor, back to her room. Serena nodded acceptance. Marlys ushered those standing around into the dining hall. Celestine sent a couple of apprentices for tea and cakes.

Since Serena already had read about Beryl and Boyd, Marlys summarized Grady's information about how sorcerers ran the world he came from. She added that he had pled for mercy from them, and told her that Argent's men who had not been felled by Kelsie had to beg Argent to heal their companions.

"He's still working at reviving his men?" Serena asked.

"According to the platter, he is," Tir said. "Though he's almost finished."

"Good," Serena said. "He'll be depleted. The time to strike is now."

"He doesn't need spells with the weapons he has," Thorne said.

"The attackers in the sorcerous wars had weapons, too," Serena said. "Yet the defenders were able to lure sorcerer leaders from underground chambers successfully on two occasions and capture them."

Thorne leaned forward in her seat. "We're listening."

"There's a calling spell, stronger than the one Clea taught us," Serena said. "With Clea's spell, a sorcerer has the choice to ignore it. With this spell, there is no choice. The spell sets a compulsion to respond."

"Like sleepwalking?" Tir asked.

Serena shook her head. "Argent would still have his wits about him. He will have the presence of mind to grab his shield and order his men around on his way to meet us. But he will come."

"What then?" Thorne said. "He'll still have the shield."

"We can separate him from the shield, as I separated him from the battle axe," Serena said.

"A distraction?" Rochelle guessed.

"I'm happy to continue to shoot arrows at him," Zaria said.

"You should," Serena said, "but there's more. Yes, we should approach him with numbers. I can create an illusion that there are many more of us. He will undoubtedly cast killer spells at us. But he will cast most of them at phantoms."

"But some of us will be solid!" Rochelle said. "We'll still be targets."

"I did not say there would be no danger." Serena said. "We can use the stakes and stay behind protective barriers to minimize the risk."

Tir gestured to Thorne. "Except for Thorne, who has been wearing the chest protector and wielding the mace."

"He will see several Thornes," Serena said. "And not be able to discern which is real."

"The shield will not block this spell?" Celestine asked.

"A spell of illusion can't be blocked," Serena said.

"How shall we proceed then?" Marlys said.

Serena turned to Marlys briefly before facing the others. "We bring six to eight sorcerers. No more. Rochelle is right. A large number of sorcerers would increase the chance that Argent will kill one of them. We set up protective barriers."

"I won't need one," Thorne said.

"Granted," Serena said. "I will cast the calling spell. Argent will emerge. He will undoubtely have the shield with him."

"I can still whack him with the mace," Thorne said.

"Not if he casts a protective spell," Tir said. "The calling spell will only summon him."

"I can cancel any protective spell," Serena said, "and he will not be aware of it. But Thorne will find herself fighting with a man much larger than she is."

"I can wear the strength belt," Thorne said.

"You can," Serena said, "but our success lies in confusion. Once I cast illusions, he will see himself surrounded. He will cast spells every which way."

"Killer spells," Rochelle said.

"Yes," Serena said. "Everyone must watch him carefully. Do not attack unless he is not looking in your direction. With attacks coming from every side, he will be distracted. I used an end point spell to appear behind him to wrench the battle axe away. I can do the same with the shield."

"A shield will be harder to take," Rochelle said.

"Use a cutting spell to slice the straps he uses to hold it," Marlys said.

"Precisely," Serena said.

"I take it anyone can get behind him," Tir said. "If you're occupied, Serena, one of us could use an end point to get close."

Serena nodded. "Or two of us, or more. Two behind him at once would increase the chances of our wrestling the shield away."

"Leaving the rest of us free to attack," Zaria said.

"It's a good plan," Rochelle said. "If it worked during the sorcerous wars, it should work for us now."

"My concern," Marlys said, "is if Argent brings his men with him. We assured Grady we would do what we could not to harm him or the other men. With Argent flinging killer spells every which way, he's almost certain to kill one of the civilians."

"We can remove them," Durand said. "I can pull a few away with the hook, one by one, even if I can't do as well as Kelsie."

"I could aim the hammer at them," Tir said, "that will cause them to flee in a panic."

Marlys nodded. "That is probably the best we can do."

"No confrontation goes exactly as planned, Marlys," Rochelle said.

"Don't I know it." Marlys took a deep breath and let it out. She looked around. "Is everyone ready to go now, or do we need time to rest and reflect further?"

"Now," Serena said.

"I agree," Rochelle said, "the best time is now."

Marlys saw nods all around. "Very well. Prepare for a battle."

Chapter 21

Tir turned to Marlys and Serena. "Who's going?"

Marlys looked around. "Besides Serena and me? If you're willing...Rochelle, Zaria, Tir, Durand, and Thorne."

All who Marlys named nodded.

Marlys turned to Nessa. "Nessa, go to Valleyview and get Janna."

Nessa immediately cast a transportation spell and disappeared.

Celestine stepped forward. "Since I'm not a combatant, I'll contact Edwina and tell her you're going to Briarhill."

"Thank you," Marlys said. "Also tell her that if she and the other Briarhill sorcerers want to observe, stay a safe distance away and use a far-seeing spell."

"I'll tell them," Celestine said, and walked away to open a sorcerous channel.

Marlys went to the armory, placed the vambrace on her arm, and picked up the mirror.

"Marlys," Thorne said as she claimed her usual weapons, "Argent's going to be casting fatal spells. If you hold up a mirror that will bounce the spell back to him, that could violate your oath not to harm another sorcerer."

"From my reading at the Library," Serena said as she took the flute, "I know of more than one case of a sorcerer bound to such an oath had cast a defensive spell where the attacker died as a result of resisting the defensive spell. The defender was unharmed."

"I'm willing to take the risk," Marlys said, "but I believe with all of my heart that the Bright Beings who bestowed the gift of sorcery did not intend for magic used in defense to result in the death of a defender."

While they were talking, Tir grabbed the hammer and the platter. Durand took the glove and the hook. Rochelle gathered the stakes and reached for the trident.

Nessa appeared with Janna.

"Thank you for taking me with you," Janna said to Marlys.

"Just don't act like a damned fool," Thorne warned.

Seeing the bludgeon had not yet been taken, Janna grabbed it. "The only person I want to see die is Argent."

Rochelle quickly explained the plan to Janna as Tir cast a locator spell and looked into the platter.

"We need to see what the state of Argent is," Tir said.

The image showed Argent sitting in what seemed to be a golden throne. He sighed. "That's everyone, Grady."

Grady bowed to him. "We are eternally grateful, venerable sorcerer."

"Good," Argent said, "I expect you to work even harder for me now. Bring me some ale...no, I need my wits about me. Bring me tea. Strong tea."

"Yes, venerable sorcerer."

The platter's image faded.

Serena turned to Marlys. "Now's the time."

Marlys cast the transportation spell.

They stepped out of the portal onto a clearing within sight of the entrance to the underground chamber. Marlys saw horses, cows, sheep, pigs, and chickens meandering among the grasses. None seemed alarmed at humans appearing nearby. Marlys guessed these were farm animals that had been taken or wandered away from their familiar meadows.

Rochelle set up three barriers facing the ground-level door, spaced so that when Argent emerged, he would be facing sorcerers from three sides. Thorne and Janna stood near the central point. Rochelle, Zaria, and Durand took position at the southernmost one. Marlys, Serena, and Tir lingered near the northernmost one.

Serena stepped away from the barrier and cast the calling spell. Tir removed the platter from the pack he had placed it in and cast a locator spell.

Marlys saw Argent rise from his chair and look around. "I have the feeling that we need to go outside, right now." He picked up his shield and motioned to his men. "Follow me."

Tir replaced the platter and took up the hammer.

Marlys raised a hand and gestured to the others. She pointed to the entrance. They all nodded in response.

Serena waited behind the barrier, poised to cast the illusion spell.

Argent emerged from the hole, shield on his left arm. His men climbed out after him, Grady in the lead.

Argent surveyed the area and spotted the sorcerers.

Thorne stepped out from behind the barrier and strode toward Argent. Immediately, Argent raised his arms and cast a spell at her. Thorne continued on her way, unaffected.

Meanwhile, Marlys saw Serena cast her illusion spell. Suddenly, it seemed that the clearing had filled with sorcerers, all copies of Marlys and her companions.

Janna, noting that Argent's attention was directed at Thorne, stepped to one side of the barrier and aimed the bludgeon. Men who had begun to run toward the sorcerers slowed their pace and stopped. Farther away, Durand used the hook to move Argent's men aside, one by one.

Tir held the hammer, but as Argent's men spread out, the animals began to move around them, making it difficult for Tir to aim clearly. Marlys knew that Tir, who had been raised on a farm, did not want to accidentally cause an animal to panic and start a stampede. Still, Tir did his best, directing the hammer to men at the edges of the group. Those men fled in panic.

Grady stayed a pace behind Argent, moving as Argent moved.

Thorne angled away from her previous path. Argent's next spell passed through an illusion of Thorne.

Zaria let loose a crossbow bolt, but Argent kept moving from side to side, trying to focus on a target, and the bolt missed.

Marlys watched Grady. Since he was behind Argent, the weapons did not affect him. But with Grady so close to Argent, there was no room for Marlys or anyone else to cast an end point spell to attack Argent from the rear. Marlys would have to leave the protective barrier to move Grady away, but felt she could hide among the animals, who had spread out and were nearing both Argent and Grady.

She made her move, weaving back and forth among the illusions to close the gap between her and Grady. Seeing Argent begin to turn in her direction, she quickly ducked behind a cow. She heard Thorne shout "I'm over here, you ass!" taking his attention away from her.

Argent raised his arms abruptly to cast another spell. The shield fell off his arm and landed at his feet. Before Argent could bend and grab it, Grady snatched it and hurried away. Marlys sprinted forward as Argent straightened and raised his arms to cast a spell. She stopped when she reached a point facing Argent, holding the mirror firmly in front of her as the spell landed. Marlys recoiled slightly at the impact, but was otherwise unaffected as Argent toppled and lay flat on the grasses.

Marlys glanced backward to confirm that Grady was still alive. Lowering the mirror, she knelt by Argent's body, placing a hand on his chest.

Marlys heard Serena's voice behind her and felt a hand on her shoulder. "Marlys, are you all right?"

Marlys stood. "Yes."

Serena gestured toward Argent. "Is he dead?"

"Yes."

"Stand back so I can dispose of the body," Serena said. "Nothing should remain of him for any followers of his to venerate."

Marlys nodded and complied. The illusions were gone. The sorcerers had gathered around. Grady lingered nearby, frozen, looking scared, still clutching the shield.

Serena took a deep breath and cast a spell at Argent. His body and clothes dissolved. Serena took out the flute and blew strongly. They heard a clear tone as a brief but violent gust of wind scattered Argent's ashes.

As Serena put the flute away, Thorne walked up to her and patted her upper arm. "Well done."

Serena nodded.

Grady edged toward Marlys. With a bow, he extended the shield to her. She accepted it.

Rochelle extended an arm. "May I see?"

Marlys handed the shield to her.

Rochelle examined the shield carefully and turned to Grady. "The fastenings for the straps were loosened. A very professional job, but they were definitely tampered with. Argent probably never even noticed until he unintentionally shook it off."

Grady took off his hat, held it to his chest, and bowed again.

"Thank you," Marlys said.

Grady looked relieved but did not answer.

Rochelle gestured at Marlys. "I used the trident to gather the men. They're all here."

Looking around, Marlys saw that the men had grouped together. Those nearest her still sat on the ground. Janna stood above them with a triumphant grin. Behind them, the remainder of Argent's men waited anxiously.

Serena stepped close to Marlys. "I have rooted them wherever they're standing and sitting. They won't be able to walk away until I release them."

Marlys cast a spell to amplify her voice. "We mean you no harm. You'll be returned to your home world, where you can go about your business."

The men's expressions varied from relief to skepticism.

"We'll be collecting your charms," Marlys continued. "Take them off, please."

Janna, Tir, and Durand began circulating among the men. All surrendered the charms without resistance. Marlys noticed Argent's men stealing wary glances at Zaria and Rochelle, who held weapons pointed at them.

Thorne touched Marlys's arm. "They need to know what's expected of them in plain language. Would you mind if I spoke to them?"

Marlys considered. Thorne would probably be harsh. Still, perhaps harshness was called for. In any case, Marlys could always contradict anything Thorne said. Glancing around, she saw Serena incline her head toward Thorne, as if to signal to let Thorne make a speech.

"Very well," Marlys said to Thorne.

Thorne faced the group and cast a spell to amplify her voice. "Listen to me. Argent is dead, as you saw for yourselves. Your days of raiding are over. Yes, I know that Argent forced you, most against your will. Whether or not you obeyed willingly, when we return you to your own world, you will all be on your best behavior. Argent will not be there, but I will, and I will make sure you follow a peaceful path."

Marlys turned to Thorne, wondering if she had heard correctly. The other sorcerers looked at her with expressions of surprise. Marlys held up her hand to delay an exclamation.

Janna grinned. "I'll be there, too!"

At that moment, sorcerers from Briarhill arrived. They formed a circle around Argent's men.

Edwina walked up to Marlys. "We saw. Argent is dead. Thank you."

"He was the agent of his own destruction," Marlys said.

"What now?" Edwina said.

Marlys gestured toward the men. "We've collected all their charms. You should be able to handle them now. They'll be returning to the island worlds. See to it that they gather whatever they brought with them and stay with them until we are ready to send them back."

"We can open a portal at any time," Edwina said.

"Yes," Marlys said. "But they need time to think about their new reality. If we send them home now, there may be chaos."

"How long?" Edwina said.

"It will take a day or two for Janna and I to get our things together," Thorne interjected.

"You're...going with them?" Edwina asked.

"Yes," Thorne said. "Someone has to. They've had a leader for a long time. A bad one. They need another leader, one who will guide them on a better path, strongly if necessary."

Durand stepped over to them. "Allow me to offer my services in the interim while they wait here. They're used to male leadership."

Edwina nodded. "We'd welcome that."

Marlys turned to Serena. "You can release Argent's men now. Durand, Edwina, and the other Briarhill sorcerers will take charge."

Serena cast the spell. The men who were sitting, stood. All of Argent's men appeared ready to cooperate.

Marlys turned to Durand. "Shall we leave some of the weapons with you?"

"Since we've collected all the charms, and Argent is no longer a threat, I think I can manage with Edwina and the other sorcerers," Durand said.

"Very well. May the Bright Beings watch over all of you." Marlys waved at the Goldenvalley sorcerers. "Come with me." She cast the transportation spell.

When they emerged at the fortress, sorcerers and the apprentices gathered around them as they returned the weapons to the armory wall.

"Is Argent dead?" Celestine asked.

"Yes," Serena said quickly before Marlys could reply.

The room broke out in cheers.

Astrid stepped forward. "Shall I spread the news to the other regions and the Library?"

"Yes, please do," Marlys said.

Astrid walked out of the audience room.

Marlys looked around. "Let's all sit. There are issues we need to discuss."

"I agree," Thorne said, and followed Marlys into the dining hall with the others.

Celestine sent the apprentices for tea and cakes while everyone else settled themselves. Tir and Rochelle took the lead in explaining how Argent had been defeated, and that his men were temporarily under the custody of Durand and the Briarhill sorcerers. By the time they had finished explaining, trays had been set on the tables and everyone had been served.

Marlys regarded Thorne, who sat across from her.

"You're wondering about my announcement that I would return to the island worlds with Argent's men," Thorne said.

Marlys heard gasps. Out of the corner of her eye, she saw Serena staring at Thorne intently, her face wearing a knowing smile.

"That was sudden," Celestine said.

Thorne faced Celestine. "Not at all. Ever since I was released from the time-bind, I've thought of going elsewhere. My time here is over. Oh, I've done my best to blend in. I admit that I've learned much in the past couple of years. In particular, I've found there are better, more effective methods to train sorcerers and interact with citizens than when I was High Sorcerer. But I've always felt awkward here. I felt I was tolerated rather than celebrated. Now I have a chance to go a place that has rules more to my liking. Argent's men need supervision. I can provide that. I can be a High Sorcerer again."

"You and Janna?" Rochelle asked.

While Thorne spoke, Nessa had been looking at her with a stunned expression. "Janna is going too?"

"Where Thorne goes, I go," Janna said. "When Thorne contacted me through the sorcerous channels and told me Grady's story, I thought that his world was just the place for me."

Throne smiled and embraced Janna in a one-armed side hug.

Nessa let out a long breath. "Since we're all saying what's on our minds, I, too, feel out of place here. Yes, the regions have rescinded my banishment, but that banishment was in place for some time. Longer than Zaria, even. I'd rather go with Aunt Thorne. They'll need a Librarian to access the treasures of the obelisk anyway."

"Two Librarians," Zaria said. "I would have been perfectly content staying here for the rest of my life, but I'm not going to remain in Goldenvalley without Nessa. We've been friends for a long time. We take meals together. If I didn't see her every day, I think my day would seem incomplete."

Nessa looked at Zaria with a wide smile.

Thorne regarded them both. "Only if you can accept me as High Sorcerer."

Zaria shrugged. "Doesn't matter to me as long as I'm with Nessa."

"I'm perfectly happy serving where you are High Sorcerer, Aunt Thorne," Nessa said.

Marlys thought that with the age gap, Nessa or Zaria would eventually succeed Thorne as High Sorcerer anyway. She spoke up. "Since we've had four express their wishes to go to the island worlds, is there anyone else?"

Deep silence answered her.

"I'll open a sorcerous channel to the entire continent later and ask if anyone else wants to go with Thorne," Marlys said after a few moments. "Thorne, can you wait a day or so?"

"Yes, I need to gather my things together. I won't be coming back."

Serena clapped her hands together. When all turned to her, she said, "Shall we have a going away party tomorrow? To send them off well? Celestine, do we have sufficient supplies to celebrate?"

Celestine smiled and nodded. "Ample supplies. I'd be happy to take charge of the arrangements."

"Then it's settled," Serena said.

"Very well," Marlys said. "Celestine, gather your team. Nessa, would you take Janna back to Valleyview to collect her things?"

"Of course." Nessa rose from her seat and left the room with Janna.

"Everyone else can go about the usual business," Marlys said.

Once the others had dispersed, Marlys approached Serena.

"Did you know about this in advance?" Marlys said.

"I knew that Thorne was never entirely happy here," Serena said. "Didn't you?"

Marlys shrugged. "I knew that she had resigned herself to her current environment. She seemed to be making the best of it."

"She was very interested in Grady's description of his world," Serena said.

"There's a difference between being interested and actually going there to live," Marlys said.

"True," Serena said. "Yet, I was not entirely surprised at her choice."

"She seems to be excited about it," Marlys said. "She may change her mind once she's there. She knows how to return."

"Universe forbid!" Serena said. "I wish her no harm, but I hope that she is so delighted to be there that she never comes back."

"That may well happen," Marlys said.

That evening, Marlys opened channels throughout the continent. She found that many places were in the midst of celebrations. They had removed the protective barriers. Already they were making plans to help the homes, businesses, and farmsteads Argent had looted rebuild and restock.

After Marlys revealed that Thorne and Janna would go to the island worlds to live, and that Thorne intended to resume her title there as High Sorcerer, eleven sorcerers expressed a wish to join them. All had been in Thorne's assembly and had been time-bound, and later released, by Marlys.

Once she had made the announcement to the continent, Marlys said farewell to her listeners and narrowed the communication to the training centers at Goldenvalley. Each had put together a feast as soon as Astrid had told them that Argent was dead. Marlys invited them all to another celebration the next day to send off the sorcerers going to the island worlds. All accepted the invitation.

When Marlys closed the channel, she sat back in her chair and sighed. The crisis had lasted only a matter of weeks, not even a year. She had had to marshal all of her resources to meet the challenge. Now, at last, she could rest. She decided to take a long hot bath before bed.

When she emerged, robed, from the bathroom, she met Thorne coming into their common room.

"Janna's settled into her guest room here with her belongings," Thorne said.

"What about you?" Marlys asked.

"I'm packed and ready to leave. More than ready."

"There are eleven of the old assembly wanting to go with you."

Thorne smiled and nodded. "I've talked to them. Sorcerous channels."

Marlys inclined her head. "Your own assembly, again."

Throne lifted her arms and stretched. "Feels wonderful."

"No doubts?"

Thorne lowered her arms and shook her head. "None. I know how to handle anyone from brigands to those who are cowed by them. From what Grady told us about their governing system, I'll have the authority."

"You still may have to answer to the sorcerers at the capital."

"I will have two Librarians with me. We'd be more than a match."

"The unexpected will still happen."

"I'm ready to rise to the challenge."

"May the Bright Beings watch over you, then. I will miss you."

Thorne chuckled. "You won't miss me. Not for a moment."

"I've come to know you. You've been part of my life for a long time, before and after. I will miss you."

"Do you regret freezing me in time?"

Marlys answered without hesitation. "No."

"Honesty," Thorne said. "Good." She took a breath. "I said it earlier and I meant it: I have learned from you, and the others here who were not of my assembly. I had a narrow vision of the world before. Now it is wider. I believe I am wiser. I will survive."

"I don't doubt it," Marlys said. "Good night."

The next day after breakfast, sorcerers and apprentices from other parts of Goldenvalley streamed into the fortress. The ones pledging to go with Thorne brought their things with them. Marlys greeted all of them at the front entrance as they came in.

There was no particular ceremony to observe. Celestine and her assistants had set up tables in the audience hall and placed food and drink there. Astrid had circulated the names of all who were going with Thorne. Looking around, Marlys saw hugs being exchanged here and there. Sorcerers gathered in small groups to extend their best wishes to those departing. The occasion was neither overly joyous nor overly gloomy. The room was abuzz with friendly conversation.

Marlys approached Thorne as a well-wisher left her.

Before Marlys could say anything, Thorne spoke up.

"I've had contact with Durand," she said. "There has been no trouble there. He describes the mood as hopeful, though some are nervous about the upcoming change in leadership in their area."

"Do you think you can manage that?"

Thorne smiled and nodded. "I can. I've told Durand that I'll take the sorcerers through first. After I go, can you contact him for me?"

"Of course."

"Durand will send the men through. I've prepared a speech in my mind. I'll simply tell them they are free to go to their homes and that I don't expect, nor will I tolerate, any trouble. If they need sorcerous help, they can come to us. We sorcerers will visit the village regularly to be sure that all is well. I think that will reassure them."

"I'm sure Durand would stay a few days to help with the transition if you wish."

"He offered," Thorne said in a congenial tone. "But I told him that I think it would be better if it was clear that I, and the sorcerers with me, will be in charge from the start. If Durand comes, they may look to him instead."

"I see your point."

Thorne touched Marlys's arm. "Then this is goodbye."

Marlys nodded toward the dais. "Let me say a word of farewell first, on behalf of those staying. Join me?"

"Yes, I have something to say, as well."

The room quieted as Marlys and Thorne ascended the steps to the platform.

Marlys faced the group. "Today we bid farewell to our friends and colleagues." She nodded to Thorne and turned back to the assembly. "May the Bright Beings watch over you and bring you good health and peace in your new endeavor."

Thorne stepped close to Marlys. "It is time for us to leave. Change happens to all, and I think this new chapter for us will be beneficial for those staying and those leaving. We, too, wish you all the best in the future. May the blessings of the Bright Beings remain with us all." She gestured to the assembly. "Those coming with me, gather your things and meet me outside."

Everyone filled the green between the fortress and the orchard. Once Thorne had gathered her group, everyone else backed away to a safe distance. Thorne turned, smiled at Marlys, and cast the spell to open the gateway to the island worlds. The maelstrom pulled them all in, and the portal closed.

Marlys opened a sorcerous channel. "Durand, Thorne and her company have gone."

"I'll send the men and join you at the fortress."

"Please do." Marlys closed the channel.

Serena raised her arms, waved, and raised her voice. "Marlys, there's still food and drink on the tables. We haven't had a victory celebration here at the fortress. What do you say to inviting our guests to stay and have one?"

Marlys smiled. "Yes." She faced the others. "Please join us in celebrating our success. We all worked for it."

She was answered by cheers. Everyone streamed back into the fortress. Tir, Rochelle, and other musicians retrieved their instruments. Many danced to the music. The atmosphere was merry.

As Marlys walked around the room, she received a number of congratulations. She was quick to acknowledge the contributions of others in defeating Argent.

Marlys hardly noticed the passing of time until the sun lowered enough to shine near the ceiling. She wandered toward a table where Serena, Rochelle, Tir, Voni, and Durand had gathered, feet up on the benches, mugs of cider in their hands. Marlys poured a mug of warm cider for herself and sat with them.

Celestine approached carrying a glass bottle of dark liquid. "Rum, anyone?"

Durand held out his mug. "I'll have a taste."

Celestine poured a small amount into his mug. Serena, Rochelle, and Voni raised their mugs. Celestine then parceled out more, a little at a time. When they had been served, Celestine poured herself a mug of cider, added a bit of rum, and sat with the rest of them.

Since Celestine had settled next to her, Marlys held out her mug. "I'd take a drop."

Celestine reached for the bottle and poured a small amount into Marlys's mug.

"This ended well," Serena said. "Argent is gone, his men have gone, and Thorne has left the building."

Tir shifted his weight in the chair. "I wasn't going to say anything, but...."

"Oh, you can say something," Marlys said. "I've been approached by others, hesitantly indicating that they're relieved Thorne went away, not that they wished her any harm of course, and hoping she's happy at her new location."

"To their and our credit," Voni said, "everyone worked hard at getting along. Elspeth seemed the most settled. But Janna, Kelsie, and others in Thorne's old assembly never seemed entirely happy here."

"An amicable parting of the ways," Durand said. "Those following Thorne's way with Thorne, those following Marlys's way with Marlys."

"Well put, sir," Serena said.

Marlys waved toward the middle of the floor, where apprentices and sorcerers continued their merrymaking. "Some of Thorne's assembly remained with us, and seem content to stay. I think that's to our credit."

Celestine lifted her mug. "May the blessings of the Bright Beings be with Thorne and her company. They'll need all the blessings the Universe can offer."

"They certainly will," Rochelle said, raising her mug.

"Now life can get back to normal," Tir said.

"Except it never does," Durand said. "But it can be a good life, nonetheless."

"May the Universe grant that it be so," Marlys said.

The End

Other books by
Joan Marie Verba

The Chronicles of the Library of Sorcery (trilogy)
   Secrets of the Sorcerers
   Clash of the Sorcerers
   Shadows of the Sorcerers
   http://libraryofsorcery.com

Summoned by Dragons: Fire and Friendship
   http://summonedbydragons.com

Twelve: A Retelling of the Twelve Dancing Princesses
   http://twelvefairytale.com

Defying the Ghosts: A Haunted House Story
   http://defyingtheghosts.com